Extra Credit

DAISY LANDISH

Editing by Rachael Lammie
Cover by Daisy Landish

BEACHES AND TRAILS
PUBLISHING

NOTE: This book was previously published as The Science Fair Trilogy (Dating Hypothesis, Dating Experiment, and Dating Conclusion)

Prologue

FERNBROOK WAS a small town nestled in the heart of the Lake District, part of the Greater West Water area that's tucked in the surrounding mountains and valleys, encircled by beautiful lakes. With barely two hundred people to call it home, it was one of those communities where everyone knows everyone else. Not that the town was stagnant and without its fair share of excitement. Fernbrook was visited a lot by tourists. They loved to rent a boat for a day and sail the smooth waters.

Sailing and hiking expeditions were the small town's primary income source. The picturesque village was beautiful all year round and featured world-famous bakeries. As the town's popularity grew, celebrities frequently visited the B&B and central hotel, Lake View Lodge. Fernbrook was perfectly located for easy access to the rest of Northern England. Even though everyone knew everyone's business and there were no secrets in Fernbrook, most residents stayed in the small town, not venturing out to the big cities.

If you wanted to relocate to Fernbrook, you had to join the waitlist. It was rare that a house or piece of land came up for sale because everyone loved the small town so much. It was not only rich in beauty but also in its community. Everyone was always happy to help each other, and the small village was one big happy family.

The pride and joy of Fernbrook was the secondary school, The Northern Swan.

Pupils from The Northern Swan boasted some of the best exam results in the country. People from up and down England applied for their kids to join, but The Northern Swan only accepted a handful of students who didn't live in Fernbrook. Some of the school's pupils went on to Oxford or Cambridge. Others travelled abroad and completed their education in the world's most prestigious schools.

Some of the school's most successful students would visit once a year for the school's open house, which showed off the school and help attract investors. Not that they were hard to find. Lawyers, business tycoons, and engineers had been nourished and flourished under the school's dedicated teachers and were more than willing to donate funds enough to make The Northern Swan a showpiece of modern education.

Unlike most UK schools, The Northern Swan took part of its curriculum from schools worldwide. Their innovative approach to teaching was touted as being the reason for the students' brilliance. In addition, they hosted a selection of extracurricular activities such as drama, sports, glee club, a choir and cheerleading, and a host of triathlons and other sporting events.

Like most schools though, The Northern Swan was not without conflict. While the teachers encouraged students to be inclusive and accepting of each other, the students preferred to stick with their cliques. They had their sports kids, mathletes, drama kids, and many more. The faculty at The Northern Swan had a zero-tolerance policy on bullying and always encouraged students from all social groups to work together. While the students complained, these tactics had proved to be a tremendous success.

In the class of 2007, two of the school's most promising students were Charlotte Black and Benedict Cookson. Charlotte and Benedict were from completely different worlds. From the moment they met, it was clear they were oil and water. No one could really say why they rubbed each other the wrong way. But it soon became apparent the only way to manage their animosity was to try to stay apart as much as possible. These feelings were made worse by their competitiveness, as each sought to attain the school's most prestigious awards. Over time, this developed into an intense dislike for each other, to where the tension between them was almost palpable if they was in the same room.

As the final year of school approached, Charlotte and Benedict were both secretly working towards the school's rewards program. If a student hit the criteria and had the suitable recommendations, the school would help them apply and get the grants needed to help them secure a place at their chosen university. The rewards program also offered a financial reward to help with studies, travel, or starting a new business. Every year, students would apply, but only a handful could be selected. Only three students could win this award per year.

As the rewards program was popular and competitive, many students kept their results close to their chest. Of course, there were plenty who bragged about their grades and odds of winning, but Charlotte and Benedict were among those who kept their cool. Maybe they each hoped their silence would be mistaken for disinterest in the award. After all, it was better to be underestimated and steal victory from what looked like the jaws of defeat.

This made them more alike than either of them would have ever admitted.

Chapter One

BENEDICT WAS AN ARROGANT IDIOT.

Well, maybe not an idiot. As much as Charlotte hated to admit it, there were very few students at The Northern Swan who were as smart as him. She'd overheard the teachers talking once that Benedict had got one of the highest IQs in the school's history.

It rather made her wonder where she fell on that list. High no doubt. But as high as him? Higher?

No. He wasn't stupid. But did Benedict really need to look down on everyone who wasn't as smart as him? Anti-social, closed minded...He judged anyone who was interested in the arts, or the other subjects he deemed a waste of time.

Charlotte, on the other hand, helped organise and host many of the school's events, and she couldn't help but notice how Benedict never got involved. Even when the school's football or rugby team celebrated their successes, he was nowhere to be found. Charlotte shook her head. His loss, her gain. In her mind, she labelled him a self-centered brat and told herself it didn't matter.

And it didn't. Not really.

Charlotte was naturally beautiful and blessed with a talent for the arts. She was tall, slim, with thick blonde hair that fell halfway down her back in a silken cascade. With her emerald-green eyes, it was only natural that she attracted the attention of the hottest guy in school and was picked as head cheerleader in her first year. It wasn't her fault that she was so talented.

Likewise, Benedict was skilled in academics, a straight-A student who was often flooded with the girls' attention from his class. Unlike Charlotte, Benedict had no interest in dating, and while Charlotte was great at sports, Benedict was rubbish at them. They were complete polar opposites and yet they were constantly compared one to the other. This irritated Charlotte, quite naturally, who failed to see just how alike they were.

Perhaps if she'd understood just how much they had in common, she might have been more forgiving of his attitude. She might have even realised that the things she hated so much about him were reflected in herself. They were, after all, a product of parents who lived their lives through their children. Both were being held to ridiculously high standards.

Was it any wonder they tried so hard and looked down on the rest of the world with so much contempt?

Charlotte's mum, Ava, was a veteran of the beauty pageant circuit and even ran her own business training girls for their beauty pageant debut. From the time Charlotte could walk and talk, Ava had pushed her ideas on her. It didn't matter that Ava was a successful business-woman. Her business had come after years of success on the circuit, so she never cared for education, seeing little value in it. Ava lived by old-fashioned values, thinking it was more important for a girl to be the perfect housewife and find a husband than be able to stand up on her own two feet.

"A girl with your beauty is rare, darling. You shouldn't let it go to waste. A real man doesn't want a woman who can outperform him in the boardroom," Ava would say.

"Mum, I don't want to depend on my husband. I want to make my own money, to do things for myself," Charlotte would argue back.

"You can do that, darling. Just look at me. Beauty fades. Make the most of it while you can. You could be the next big model. Then you could have any man you want and be financially independent. Master the beauty pageant circuit as I did. That's the first stepping-stone to modelling," Ava would respond, clearly not about to back down.

It was often a source of conflict at home. Charlotte wanted to make her mother proud, and truth be told, she enjoyed the beauty pageants and casting calls for modelling shoots. It broke her heart when she had to hide her academic successes from her mother. Charlotte was often jealous of her friends' relationships with their mothers, but that didn't stop her from loving Ava all the same. Their relationship was just different from most.

One thing that vexed Charlotte the most was that many people considered her obsessed with her looks.

Well, this wasn't entirely untrue, not if she were honest with herself. As a result, people frequently underestimated her. People would overlook her, assuming that she wouldn't be interested in some events or subjects. As Charlotte grew older, she tried to not let this bother her so much. She actually started liking when people underestimated her. She lived for the look of surprise on their faces when she proved them wrong.

Yet nothing got under her skin more than when Benedict would talk down her successes as if her achievements were less than his.

"Well done, Charlotte. I hope you are applying for the rewards program. With grades like these and your extracurricular activities, you have a real shot at winning," one of her teachers, Mrs Bran, had said one day after handing Charlotte her history assignment back.

Charlotte looked over the paper to see a large A+ stamped into the top corner and comments of praise in the margins of each page.

Charlotte smiled. "Thanks, Mrs Bran!"

Benedict was sitting in the seat in front of Charlotte and mumbled something she couldn't hear.

"Say something?" she asked, giving his chair leg a swift kick under the table.

"Whatever," Benedict replied, turning his paper over. He didn't turn it fast enough for Charlotte not to notice his A and a ninety-eight percent in the top corner.

It shouldn't have, but it gave her a tiny smidge of satisfaction that she has scored higher than the school's genius. It gave her even more satisfaction that he seemed to know it too. She wondered sometimes if things would have been different somehow, more rewarding if they'd been friends. They'd never been able to manage it though. Charlotte could hardly remember saying more than a few sentences to Benedict once she thought about it. All the same, the pair continuously clashed for some reason.

What made it even more irritating was just how much their feud was a source of grand entertainment for the rest of the school. Something needed to change.

Chapter Two

BENEDICT THOUGHT LITTLE MORE of Charlotte than she did of him. He felt she was self-absorbed and a bit of an airhead, forever living in her dream world. Benedict assumed Charlotte thought she was better than everyone else and wasted far too much time with her extracurricular activities such as drama and cheerleading. Cheerleading was more of an American activity, and Benedict could never understand why Charlotte, and the school, took part in the sport.

Benedict's father, Robert, much like Ava, was stern and humourless. Yet, unlike Ava, Robert prized education and knowledge above anything else. For as long as Benedict could remember, his schoolwork was criticised, with Robert always pushing him to do more and to be better than everyone else.

"YOU CAN DO BETTER than this. Show me you're not as stupid as you're pretending to be. Now re-read it!" Robert's voice boomed as he shoved heavy books at the boy, classical literature and history years above the child's understanding.

"Robert, stop. He is four years old. Let him be a child, for God's sake," Clara snapped, scooping a crying Benedict into her arms.

"No son of mine will be an idiot!" Robert yelled back.

"With a father like you, can you blame him?"

"He should read at a higher level. When I was his age, I could read twice as fast as he does now and was already halfway through the collected works of Shakespeare!" Robert yelled, tossing the book forcefully across the room.

"Really? And all the reading, what exactly has it done for you? It certainly didn't teach you compassion or human decency. He is barely out of diapers for crying out loud," Clara screamed back as she cradled a now hysterical Benedict.

ROBERT'S DEMANDS on Benedict to do better, and his temper when Clara disagreed, was the primary source of conflict during his parents' brief marriage. Benedict never asked what their relationship was like before he was born. As far back as he could remember, all they did was argue. At first, Benedict tried to do better to please his father and stop his yelling. When that didn't work, he tried everything he could to show his parents how much he loved them. But everyone had their breaking point, and the arguments eventually became too much for his mother to bear. Clara left when Benedict was five.

Benedict was entirely unprepared for this abandonment. Clara had always showered Benedict with love and affection. He never could figure out why she had left him behind. Maybe his father was right, and he wasn't good enough after all. It didn't help that Robert blamed Benedict for Clara's leaving, telling his son that she would have stayed if he had been smarter and done better in school. As Benedict grew older, he knew his father's words were said in grief, but it didn't stop them from hurting.

His father's words plagued him for years. With only his father in his life, he pushed himself to do better, to be smarter than everyone else. Constantly fearful his father would leave him too if he were not good enough, he would study late into the night when he got home from school, double-checking and triple-checking his work. In school, he would sit anxiously waiting for the results until he felt sick to his stomach from the stress.

At home, his father would look over his shoulder, pushing him to plan what he would do when he won the rewards program.

"Look at the past winners. Do you see any of them with grades any less than an A+? No! you're slipping, boy!" Robert scolded, looking down his nose at his son.

"I'm trying, dad. I have the highest IQ in the school's history."

"I know, son. That's why I am so hard on you. You have a rare gift, and you're letting it go to waste. What good is a high IQ if you don't put it to work?" Robert said.

Benedict thought his father sounded sorry for snapping, but it was short-lived before the demands and insults started in again. All Benedict ever wanted was his father's approval, a hug, or a simple 'well-done son, I'm proud of you.' But it never came.

It annoyed Benedict how Charlotte seemed to match his results, especially given how much hard work he put into his grades. He was convinced she was using her looks to bribe some of the other students to do her work. She was quiet in class, but always seen laughing and joking with her friends everywhere else she went. She spent so much time working on pageants, casting calls, and school events that Benedict couldn't understand how she was doing so well.

It's not fair. I put in all this work, and she does nothing for the same results.

What was worse was how everyone praised Charlotte when she did well, while everyone expected the boy-genius to perform purely because of his IQ. Everyone assumed it came naturally to him, and while that was partly true, it annoyed him that no one knew just how much effort he spent.

"Wonder who she got to write that one for her," Benedict mumbled, rolling his eyes at Mrs Bran's praise.

"Say something?" Charlotte asked, kicking his chair.

Chapter Three

THE BELL RANG, punctuating the end of history class and that the students should quickly head to their next session. Benedict shoved his paper in his bag, cramming it deep down, trying to forget about it. His father wouldn't be happy when he saw his results. He expected nothing less than 100% every single time.

Tossing his bag over his shoulder and grabbing his blazer, he practically ran out the door and down the hall. His science class was on the third floor, and already a stream of students gathered at the lifts, too lazy to take the stairs. Taking the stairs two at a time, Benedict pushed his way through the chattering students and stormed into the empty science room. Tucking himself in a corner at the back of the room, he buried his head in his book and waited for class to start.

Charlotte was one of the last students to join the class just before the bell rang. Benedict tried to ignore her and not let her get to him, but he felt his blood boil as she entered the classroom, laughing and joking with the other cheerleaders as though she hadn't a care in the world. *Some have it so easy,* he thought.

"Everyone, settle down. I have news and need your full attention," the science teacher, Mr Smythe, said in his usual chipper tone.

The students settled and sat, waiting patiently for his announcement. Mr Smythe was one of the most popular teachers in the school. The students loved him, and he had such a passion for education that he kept the students enthralled.

"Now, as I am sure you are all aware, the school has wanted to expand its science program for some time now. Well, I am happy to announce that we have joined the regional science fair for the first time!" He cheered, and the students cheered with him.

"Unfortunately, not all will get to compete, which I think is a shame because you are all the best students a teacher could ask for," he said, bowing his head and placing his hand over his heart.

"Sir, I bet you say that to all your students," Charlotte said and chuckled, causing her friends to laugh with her.

"What's the criteria for entry, Sir?" Benedict interrupted, wanting to get to the critical information and enjoying the annoyed look Charlotte's friends shot him.

"I'm glad you asked. Luckily, it's only open to year elevens, so thankfully, you all can submit an application," the teacher began, tucking his arms behind his back. He paced the room. "With it being a regional event, at least fifteen schools compete. Each of you will be teamed up based on your grades to create the best teams. You have a month to come up with an experiment or project of your choosing. After that, I need a detailed paper explaining your project, and the best two will be picked," he finished, and the students groaned their complaints.

"Sir, we have been waiting for this for years. Only two? It's not fair," Benedict complained, and his classmates agreed with him.

"Settle down, class. I know it's not fair, but we have to prove why we deserve to be invited back next year as it's our first event. Once we have proven ourselves, they will invite more students. I believe in you all. So please don't make this an easy job for me," Mr Smythe said, scanning the room with a stern look, letting his students know how serious he was.

"I will put up the pairings sheet at the end of the day when I have reviewed the best teams. Now, onwards and upwards. Open your books to where we last left off....A certain physics problem, I believe," he chirped, turning to the whiteboard, and beginning to write up the day's lesson.

The students went about their day debating who they thought Mr

Smythe would pair up with whom. Benedict tried to forget it, not needing the distraction. He'd know this soon enough. Instead, he needed to concentrate on the rest of his classes that day, so he could do his best. But at the back of his mind, he worried about how his father would react to his less than perfect score on the history test. He wound up trying to distract himself by coming up with ideas for the science fair. He hoped he would be paired up with Simon. He was the only one Benedict could think of whose intelligence matched his own. Plus, Simon had a string of success in other subjects and came from a long line of electrical engineers, meaning they could be sure to come up with something interesting.

In the meantime, Charlotte was also worried about whom she would be paired up with. She had spent so long hiding her intelligence that she didn't want anyone to think of her as a geek. She had a reputation to protect. So instead, she busied herself through the day with cheerleading practice and music class, pretending the science fair was the furthest thing from her mind.

Three-thirty rolled around quicker than expected. Time had a way of flying when you are having fun. The last bell rang, and the year eleven students ran to the science lab searching for the name of whom they were to be partnered with.

"You have got to be kidding me!" Benedict groaned louder than he intended as he read the name paired with his own, causing several students to stare at him in alarm. He didn't wait around to see their reactions. Benedict stormed into Mr Smythe's classroom demanding answers only to find Charlotte had already beat him to it. As the door burst open, she eyed Benedict with annoyance for a long moment and turned her attention back to Mr Smythe.

"Sir, this has to be a mistake," she protested, her hands on her hips in what could only be described as a combative stance.

"It's no mistake," Mr Smythe replied, leaning back in his chair, and peering over his glasses that slid down the end of his nose.

"Sir, I'm sorry, but I can't work with her. The rewards program is on the line. I have no chance of winning if I'm forced to work with her!" Benedict argued, taking advantage of the pause to express his own point of view before this could go any further.

"Excuse me? What about me? Being forced to work with you?" Charlotte spat back.

"Oh please, you should be begging to be paired up with me. Any chance you have of winning lies with me. But that doesn't mean I should be forced to work with *you*. Some of us have a future. A real future to think about," Benedict retorted.

Charlotte felt her blood boil. She clenched her fists at her side to stop herself from slapping Benedict square in the face. "What the heck is that supposed to mean? You don't even know me. How dare you assume such things about me!" Charlotte yelled.

"Oh pipe down, prom queen," Benedict snarled.

The pair continued to argue and shout, causing a small crowd to gather outside the lab watching the show through the open doorway. Cell phones came out.

"Enough!" Mr Smythe yelled and levelled a glare at participants and spectators alike.

Charlotte and Benedict fell silent, and the students at the door dispersed. Mr Smythe never raised his voice. He was the bubbly teacher, always happy and chipper. Benedict and Charlotte shared a look, both not knowing what to do at the sudden outburst of their favourite teacher.

"Do you two doubt my skills as a teacher?" Mr Smythe asked.

The pair shook their heads wordlessly.

"So why do you doubt me now? I don't know where this childish conflict has come from, and frankly, I don't care. You two have the best test scores in your form. If anyone has a chance of winning the fair, gaining praise for the school, and winning the rewards program, it is you two. Imagine what you could do if you combined your skills?" Mr Smythe said calmly, steepling his fingers and waiting for a response.

Benedict and Charlotte exchanged a look of equal disapproval and disdain.

"I'm sorry, Sir, but I want another partner," Benedict said, keeping his eyes locked on Charlotte as he eyed her from head to toe.

Charlotte clenched her jaw to save from speaking her mind. *Pompous jackal*, she thought as she let her eyes travel him in return. She turned her nose up at his ripped jeans and concert t-shirt that looked three sizes too big and was covered in equal amounts of tears as his jeans.

"Everyone else is assigned. If you refuse to work together, then, unfortunately, you can't be part of the fair," Mr Smythe said with a mischievous grin on his face.

Charlotte hummed her annoyance and stormed towards the door.

She might have left the room, but Mr Smythe clearly wasn't done. He levelled a look at Benedict. He was no longer smiling, his expression serious. "I shall give you two to the end of the week. If by then you truly can't work together, let me know, and I will withdraw you from the fair."

"That's not going to happen, Sir," Benedict said confidently. While he hated Charlotte and working with her would surely be fresh heck, his long-term goals outweighed the pain of working with her.

"As I expected. I'm excited to see what you both come up with," Mr Smythe said, dismissing Benedict with a wave of his hand. "Now get out of here and get to work!"

WEEKS LATER, the whole thing finally blew up.

"It's hopeless. The math doesn't add up. It's too late to change our project. Mr Smythe has already approved our application. If we mess up now, we lose our place in the fair. I knew this would happen," Benedict bellowed as he paced his garage.

Benedict flat out refused to do the project at Charlotte's house. After a lot of arguing and failed attempts to complete the project at school, it was settled that they would work out of his dad's garage.

"I can get the math to work. Calm down! You're giving me a headache," Charlotte protested as she scribbled notes and tapped away at the calculator cradled in her hand.

"Ha! If I can't do the math, you certainly can't," Benedict scolded, plunking himself onto the chair he had pulled from the dining room.

Charlotte ripped out a page from her notebook and strode across the room, shoving the page in Benedict's face. She delighted in his surprise when he read her calculations and found them correct.

"Keep underestimating me. I love seeing that dumbfounded look on your face." She grinned, heading back to the table filled with notes, half-built components, and tools.

Benedict started at the page. He couldn't figure out how she had done the maths when he couldn't. If it were anyone else, he would be impressed. But this was Charlotte, which only vexed him more.

After much deliberation and research regarding past winners of the regional science fair, they had done their project around renewable energy. They had made boards detailing the best places for wind farms and new structural improvements for solar panels. They worked out how to make these energy sources more cost-effective and accessible to the average Joe and the impact it would have over a twenty-year period. But their main project, which they had the most issues with, was their scale models of a renewable energy plant. For some reason, the solar panel they created would short out the electrical system whenever they tried to hook it up to the light display it was supposed to turn on. Worse, the miniature wind turbine, when they could get it working, would overheat. They had to restart several times after their project caught fire. Charlotte hoped now she had got the maths to work, it would no longer be an issue. Benedict was better with the soldering, so she was happy to leave him to that. She hadn't taken the technology class that year and was regretting it.

"Oh, no you don't! It will ruin your nails. How are you to go to casting calls with hands battered and bruised from manual work?" Ava argued when she'd seen Charlotte's proposed class schedule at the beginning of the year. One call to the school office sorted out the mess. No technology class for Charlotte. Ever.

Charlotte worried that even though the project idea had been fifty-fifty, and she had figured out the maths, the main issue was with the circuitry. She didn't want Benedict taking full credit simply because he could weld.

By the end of the month, Charlotte and Benedict made a better effort to tolerate each other. Everyone could almost say they were getting along. Robert even stopped in a few times to see how they were managing. He seemed impressed with the project, and Benedict thrived, pushing himself harder. *Finally, he is happy. I've done enough. I've made him proud,* Benedict thought as his father smiled at the work they had done.

"This is some pretty complicated math. I don't think I could have figured all this out," Robert said as he scanned their paperwork.

"Thank you, Sir, it took a while," Charlotte said as she passed Benedict some more glue.

Robert's face dropped, and his eyes grew dark as he glared at Benedict. Charlotte looked between father and son with confusion.

"*You* figured out the math?" he asked.

"Well, it was a team effort. I wouldn't have known where to begin if not for Benedict's equations. And now Benedict has figured out the electrical problem," Charlotte said, feeling like she needed to explain.

"You're slipping boy, needing a cheerleader to help with basic maths," Robert said as he stared down at his son, his mouth twisted in distaste as if he'd just eaten something sour.

Benedict dropped his head. For the first time, Charlotte noticed the visible tension in his shoulders.

"It's far from basic, Sir," Charlotte shot back, hoping to defuse the situation. The atmosphere had grown grim, and Charlotte's chest felt tight and anxious.

"And now she fights your battles for you. Cat got your tongue, boy? So pathetic," Robert spat, shooting Charlotte a dark look before leaving the garage in a huff, slamming the door behind him.

"Is he always like that?" Charlotte asked, genuinely concerned for Benedict.

His jaw clenched, and he said nothing. Instead, he got up and stomped around the room, slamming drawers in the tool chest, acting like she wasn't there.

"Here, let me help," she said, reaching for the hot glue gun. Benedict snatched it away, but a blob of glue landed on his hand, causing him to cry out in pain.

"Are you ok?" Charlotte gasped, grabbing a hand towel and a water bottle from the cooler, reaching for his wrist so that she might treat his hand.

Benedict pulled away, cradling his burnt hand to his chest and glaring Charlotte down. His look was so dark and cold that it caused Charlotte to take a step back in alarm.

For a moment he looked like his father.

"You shouldn't have said anything. Now he thinks you did all the work. You may have worked out the math, but *I'm* the one doing all the proper work," Benedict snapped. He turned away and cleaned off his hand, wincing in pain when he touched the raw skin. Charlotte couldn't help but notice how quickly it had blistered. Her stomach churned at the sight of the burn.

"Excuse me? It's a joint effort. It's not my fault your dad is an uptight jerk." Charlotte snapped.

"Don't you dare talk about my dad like that!" Benedict roared.

"How can you stick up for him after the way he spoke to you?" she asked, barely holding back tears.

"I don't need your pity. Go, home cheerleader. I'm sure there is some reality TV garbage that would occupy your mind more," Benedict snarled.

"Hey! That's enough! I'm just as smart, if not smarter, than you. This project would be nothing without my input. We built this project together," Charlotte shouted, her emotions finally getting the better of her.

"Just go home. I don't need your help anymore," Benedict turned his back on her, burying his head in the notes she'd so meticulously made.

Stunned and still fighting tears, Charlotte stood and watched for a while. When Benedict did not speak to her or apologize for his and his father's cruel words, she finally grabbed her things and left.

Chapter Four

"CHARLOTTE! Charlotte, come quick. Oh, my days, this is amazing! Truly amazing!" Ava cheered, dancing around the hallway in excitement.

Charlotte ran downstairs, tugging on her denim jacket as she did and flinging her schoolbag over her shoulder.

"What's going on?" she asked her mother. "I have to get to school!"

"Come, quick," Ava chimed, grabbing Charlotte's hand and dragging her through the house to her home office in the nook just off the kitchen.

Ava shoved Charlotte in front of the large computer screen and pushed her forcefully down into the plush leather office chair. Charlotte looked at the screen, her hand going to her mouth in awe. Ava had received an email offering Charlotte a spot to audition for London's biggest modelling agency, Central Faces. She was expected the following morning at eight-thirty.

"It's everything you have been working for. Oh, darling, this is so exciting. Think of the doors this will open! I will book the train tickets; we have to get to London right away. We're going to have to go shopping and get you some new clothes. And I think we'll want to book an appointment at a salon. I have some great contacts in London. This could be the start of your career!" Ava rambled in excitement, already tapping away at her phone and making the arrangements.

Charlotte stared at the screen, not entirely sure what to say. She hadn't expected to feel this conflicted. This was a tremendous opportunity, and while she never truly wanted to be a model, the money she would earn from a few decent jobs could help pay for university and start her life the way she wanted to. She would no longer be restricted by her mother's wants and or forced to live by her expectations. Nevertheless, her heart sank when she realised the date on the invitation.

"Mum, I can't go. It's the science fair today. I've been working on this project for a month. I have a real shot at winning the school's rewards program if I win," Charlotte said, looking up at her mother in dismay.

"You must be joking. Darling, tell me you are joking? If you don't go, you will never get an opportunity like this again. Think about the doors this could open! The rewards program will be nothing compared to the money you could earn modelling," Ava argued.

"But mum..."

Ava's face grew grave, which Charlotte didn't see often. "No arguing. You are going. I am your mother, and while you live under my roof, you abide by my rules. I have put my life's work into training you, getting you ready for this exact moment. Now go pack. Our train leaves in two hours," Ava snapped, leaving Charlotte alone with the email and her conflicting thoughts and feelings.

Charlotte took out her phone and stared at her screen, trying to figure out what to say to Benedict. She typed her message two? Three times? She lost count.

Then his words flashed across her mind. She remembered the look he had given her before she'd left his house that last time. And how he had dismissed her contributions. She drifted upstairs and paced around her room, ignoring her mum's slam on the bedroom door and call for her to hurry lest they be late. Finally, she fired off a text, grabbed her bag, and followed her mum to the car.

What else could she do?

Something's come up. I can't make it. Our project is going to win, I know it. Good luck. - C

BENEDICT GROANED AT HIS PHONE, turning it over and placing it back on the kitchen table. He was glad he didn't have to deal with Charlotte, but he knew he couldn't do the presentation without her. She had figured out the math, after all. If he was asked questions about their calculations, how could he ever explain what they had done?

"What is it?" Robert asked, not looking up from his morning paper as he took a sip of his coffee.

"Charlotte can't make it to the fair. So I have to do the presentation without her," Benedict said, his voice barely above a whisper.

Robert slammed down his cup and dropped his newspaper to the floor. His face was awash with excitement.

"This is wonderful news! You can win the fair on your own. You don't have to share credit with that airhead anymore. Once you win, you will be a shoo-in for the rewards program!" Robert exclaimed, clearly pleased by the news.

This was the first time Benedict had seen his father so excited. Benedict couldn't lie. The idea of taking all the credit was tempting. He'd been working towards the reward program since his first day of school. It was what he wanted more than anything. No. It was what both he and his father wanted. That reward would allow him to go to a university of his choosing, and he could use the prize money to kick start his tech business. But Benedict's conscience niggled at the back of his mind. He couldn't take credit for what was a joint effort.

Could he?

"It's not my work, dad. We did it together. Besides, she did the math, not me."

"So what? She chose not to be here. I've looked over the math myself. I couldn't believe she had figured it out. It was fairly complicated, so I will let you off for not knowing it. Look," Robert said, running to the living room and back.

He shoved a bunch of papers in front of Benedict. Benedict realised the math was more straightforward than he thought as he looked over them. His father explained it differently than Charlotte had, and it suddenly all made sense. Excitement rushed through him. His future plans were still in his grasp.

"Study hard, son. I will go load up the car. I will be right by your side. This is so exciting! You are making school history," Robert said, finishing the rest of his almost cold coffee in one gulp and rushing off.

BENEDICT AND ROBERT arrived at the fair early. It was held at the Manchester arena. The last time Benedict had been to the arena had been two years prior when he and his friend Simon had visited Comic Con. The arena was set into sections just like then, with stalls and tables full of influential speakers discussing all the projects. There easily had to be almost three hundred people in attendance, and suddenly Benedict felt his mouth and throat go dry. He had never been one for public speaking and worried he might get stage fright. Then and there, he really wished Charlotte was there with him. He was generally happy to speak to crowds as long as someone else started and he could chime in. How in the world would he do this on his own?

"Look, there is your headteacher," Robert said, tilting his head in Mrs Cameran's direction.

"Good afternoon. I'm excited to see what you and Charlotte have come up with. Mr Smythe gave me a hint, and it sounds exciting," the headteacher said as she shook Benedict and Robert's hands.

"Charlotte couldn't make it today, Ma'am," Benedict said as he and his father assembled the project.

"Oh, what a shame," Mrs Cameran said, her face falling with disappointment.

"No need to worry, my son here is more than capable of presenting the project on his own. He did most of the work anyway," Robert said with a smile, clapping Benedict around the shoulders hard enough to make him jump.

Benedict finished setting up the experiment with his dad, his nerves growing as the rest of the students set up their projects at the surrounding tables. His pulse raced as the speaker on stage announced that the judges—a selection of headteachers from the previous five years' winners—were about to start their room tour.

"I'm going to check out the competition. I will be back before the judges get to your table," Robert said, clapping Benedict on the shoulder again.

As Benedict watched his father look over the other exhibits, he finally allowed himself to breathe. He was nervous enough about the fair. His father's presence had his anxiety levels hitting an all-time high. Hopefully, he'd stay away until after he was done talking.

Benedict talked about his project with everyone who stopped at his table, giving a short, prepared speech to anyone who asked. Everyone seemed really impressed, and a small crowd formed. Pushing their way to the front of the group were Amanda and Stacie, Charlotte's cheerleading buddies. They disregarded Benedict but admired the project knowing their friend had worked on it too.

"She's so lucky. I bet she is having so much fun. I'm not jealous at all," joked Stacie.

"Me too. I can't wait for her to get back and tell us how it went," Amanda chimed in.

Are they talking about Charlotte? Benedict listened in to their conversation as best he could while keeping the attention of all the other students discussing his project. Then, he heard the words *casting,* London and *model.* Finally, curiosity got the better of him and he pulled himself away from the crowd to take them aside.

"Hey, do you know where Charlotte is? She said she couldn't make it. I hope she isn't sick," Benedict said, hoping he was hiding his true feelings well.

Amanda and Stacie shared a look before laughing and rolling their eyes at him.

"Sick? No, Charlotte doesn't get sick. She's in London. She got an audition to be Central Faces' new model," Amanda said, hooking her arm in Stacie's and pulling her away.

Audition? She's blown off the project for an audition? His temper flared. *She knew I couldn't do the math without her. I knew she was self-absorbed. I had been right about her all along.*

He made his way back to the table just as his father approached along with the judges. *So she was willing to let me fail, ruining my future, just for a stupid modelling audition? Dad was right; I can do this without her.*

He shook off his thoughts and focused his mind. Thanks to his father, he now understood the math, and he knew he was more than capable of presenting on his own. So, while his father stood by beaming with pride, Benedict smiled and walked the judges through the presentation and demonstrated the model of the plant. He finished with the ethical, environmental, and financial benefits of renewable energy.

"I have to say I am very impressed. This has to be one of the best submissions I have seen at this fair. Well done, Benedict," beamed one judge before they moved on.

"You have got this, son. I can feel it!" Robert said, pulling Benedict in for a hug.

Benedict was taken back by his father's show of affection but found he wanted it more than even the science fair win. He wrapped his arms around his dad and soaked in the warmth of his father's embrace. *Charlotte bailing is the best thing she could have done for me.*

CHARLOTTE ARRIVED back home on Sunday morning. The audition had been an immense success, and they offered her a spot then and there. Ava had burst out crying with joy, and Charlotte had to admit that she was happy. Between the science fair, rewards program, and her new modelling job, she had several good options for the future. More than most students had. So, she bounced around the house with a newfound excitement for the things to come. *I wonder how the science fair went;* she thought as she settled in for lunch with her mother.

She scrolled through her phone and found a picture on social media stating The Northern Swan had won the fair in their first year taking part. The image attached was of headmistress Mrs Cameran shaking hands with Benedict. Their project, along with a golden trophy, was perched on the table next to him. Attached to the post was a link to an article about the fair from the local news. Excitement and pride left Charlotte feeling like she might burst at the seams. She clicked the link.

Her heart sank as the large headline screamed out at her.

Boy-genius, does it again. Leading the way for future students and setting the bar with The Northern Swan's first win at the science fair.

Charlotte sat bolt upright as she continued to read. Her stomach knotted, and bile rose in her throat. She had dealt with people she called friends being mean to her in the past. She'd even had a friend kiss a boyfriend of hers once. Yet she had never felt a betrayal like this. The article detailed how Benedict had come up with the project and created the model from start to finish. At the bottom was an interview with him. He had claimed sole responsibility and credit for the entire project. Charlotte was furious that he had left her name off the project. Her head spun at the impact it would have on her possibility of winning the rewards program. But most of all, she felt betrayed, heartbroken, and sadder than she could ever remember being. Her emotions startled her. Above all, she was upset with Benedict. Why had he disregarded her contributions? Why had he disregarded *her*? She felt used, and new anger swelled within her as she viciously swiped away tears that fell freely down her face.

Without a word to her mother who yelled after her, she grabbed her phone and stormed out, slamming the door hard behind her. Her emotions drove her onwards. She stormed past the bus stop, too wrought up to wait for the next bus, and instead walked the five miles from her house to Benedict's. After the first mile, aching feet in her high-heeled ankle boots added fuel to her anger and frustration.

She slammed on the front door, pounding her fists against the wood, and when no one answered quickly enough, she kicked at the bottom of the door.

"What the heck is wrong with you?" Benedict snapped as he flung the door open.

"Me? *Me?* What the heck is wrong with *you*?! I can't believe you would take credit for OUR project. I put just as much work into it as you. The idea for renewable energy was *my* idea. You wanted to replicate the previous year's winner. That win was just as much mine as yours, yet you didn't even acknowledge me." Charlotte screamed, waving the article in front of his face, tears flowing again down her face.

Benedict yawned and stretched, seeming unconcerned. "How was the audition?" he asked.

Charlotte was stunned. *How did he know? Was that why he'd done it?* Her mind raced.

"Not that it's any of your business, but it went great," she shot back, her response interrupted by Benedict's smug grin as he folded his arms and leaned against the door frame.

"Then what's the issue? You clearly had more important things to do. You chose not to be there on the day of the fair. I had to do the presentation alone. Therefore, I won," he said.

"You couldn't even do the basic math without me," she snapped back.

"Oh, it was far from basic, but I figured it out," Benedict lied. He wasn't prepared to admit he needed his dad's help.

"Why Benedict? I know we don't exactly like each other, but I would never do to you what you did to me!"

He pushed off from the door frame, no longer able to feign indifference. If anything, he was mad and felt he had every right to be. "What do you care? Your future is set, you wanted to be a model, and you did what you needed to do. It's a win-win, Cheerleader."

Charlotte hated how Benedict and his father used the word 'cheerleader' as an insult. She was more, so much more than just a cheerleader and a pretty face. This project had been her chance to prove that. She'd grown tired of living by everyone else's assumptions and expectations of her. She stared back at Benedict, who stood with his smug expression and, without thinking, she pulled her arm back and slapped him with all her might.

"I hope you made your father proud," she croaked, her voice breaking as she turned away.

Not that she cared if he saw her cry. In fact, she wanted him to see. She wanted him to know what he had done and how much of a low-life he was for making her feel that way.

Chapter Five

AFTER WINNING The Northern Swan's rewards program, Benedict headed off to Oxford University. After graduating, he started his own tech business following his father's plans, but he wasn't happy. A part of him always felt like something was missing. He wasn't on the path his life was supposed to be on.

Benedict moved back home to take care of Robert when he got sick. Robert, being a proud man, found plenty to complain about. Benedict's life was miserable. As a result, Benedict took the focus off his business, and after two years, he was forced to close the business. Robert made it very clear to his son how he thought he was a failure and a disappointment.

"I've wasted my life trying to make you a success. Is this the thanks I get?" he had complained.

Robert may not have been happy, but Benedict never felt freer. He'd hated the business and only did it to make his father happy. But nothing made Robert happy. Yet Benedict stayed bitter until the end.

After Robert's funeral, Benedict reconnected with some of his old friends from school.

"Hey, I don't know if it will interest you, but we are looking for a deputy head at The Northern Swan. Here is the head's number. Call her," Simon told him.

"I don't know. I've never thought about teaching. I don't even have teaching qualifications," Benedict said, staring down at the card.

He had never thought about it, but he couldn't ignore the butterflies in his stomach at the idea. Qualifications wouldn't be hard to get. One thing he had gained from his father was his thirst for knowledge and he'd taken some classes at college, which could prove to be to his advantage if he pursued this. He knew he would definitely be a better teacher than Robert ever was.

"When has The Northern Swan ever been a conventional school? Compare us to other schools across the UK, and you will see. Our curriculum is more expansive than most, our teaching methods are not the same as the rest either. However, one thing that can't be argued with is our success. Ninety-seven percent of our students move on to be super successful. Our test results are legendary, and we have won the science fair every year since your win fifteen years ago!"

Simon's enthusiasm was catching. Simon had become the school's science teacher straight from university. Science had always been his favourite subject, and he had a natural act for teaching. In addition, he had been the go-to student for mentoring back when they'd attended school together.

"I will think about it, thanks," Benedict said, surprised by how excitement grew within him at the idea.

It didn't take Benedict long. Three days later, he called and set up a meeting with the headteacher Mrs Brown, another student he attended the school with. After a tour and a month's worth of tests, shadowing other teachers, and another month of training, Benedict was welcomed as the deputy headteacher and the head of business studies.

For the first time since Benedict could remember, he felt like he was whole. He never would have thought it, but teaching was what he was meant to do. The students loved him, and he loved the students. The Northern Swan indeed was a special school.

WHEN CHARLOTTE FINISHED her last year at The Northern Swan, she and Ava moved to Kent so Charlotte could spend her time completing modelling gigs under the guidance of Central Faces. Ava handed the majority of control of her pageant preparation to her business partner and best friend, Lorraine, so she could focus on coaching Charlotte. However, a year into her modelling career, Charlotte and Ava's relationship hit a breaking point.

"Enough, Mother, you are making me miserable," Charlotte cried as she sat in her walk-in wardrobe, surrounded by pictures of herself that her mother had put up to inspire her that these previous photoshoots were inadequate.

"Don't be so ungrateful. You wouldn't have this career if it wasn't for me. Look at this beautiful house. What other girls your age would do. Do you know anyone who can say she could buy a house like this at twenty? Look at all your nice things, at these clothes. It's all because of me!" Ava argued.

"I'm not ungrateful, but Ava, this is your dream, not mine. I wanted to go to university. I wanted more from my life than to be a prize on some man's arm. And don't think I don't know about all the men you have promised me too." Charlotte yelled back as she jumped to her feet and stormed out of the room.

"How dare you call me Ava? You shall address me as mum or mother," Ava yelled as she followed her daughter through the house.

"That's the point you pick up on?" Charlotte yelled, exhausted from the constant arguing.

Every day Ava picked apart what she ate, how she sat, how she posed. Anything that could be criticized, was. Charlotte had never suffered from confidence issues before, but she felt her mental health taking a hit of late. She hated her life, and as much as she didn't want to, she was hating her mother.

"You should thank me. I have several dates for you lined up with some of London's most eligible bachelors. They wouldn't even notice you if it wasn't for the career I helped you build," Ava snapped.

"I don't want them, mum. Finding a husband and living a life from the 1950s is what YOU want, not me. Do you have any idea how smart I am? I do have a mind of my own, you know, and I'd like to do something more with it." Charlotte began tossing her mother's belonging into a large suitcase.

"What are you doing?" Ava shrieked, grabbing at her things almost frantically.

"I've had enough. Enough of you, enough of Central Faces. All of it. I want you out. I'm done, Ava!" Charlotte said, squaring her shoulders and tearing back into her mother. She felt more assertive and more sure of herself than she ever had.

It was an ugly mess. Ava showed Charlotte a new darker, more spiteful side to her than Charlotte had ever seen. Her words cut like a knife, and Charlotte sank into herself, ignoring calls and locking herself away in her house for almost six months after her mother had left. She began drinking, and when she was at her lowest, she referred herself to a therapist. It was the wake-up call she needed to get her life back on track. She sold her house and moved to a cosy little flat in central London while she completed her psychology degree.

Chapter Six

FIFTEEN YEARS LATER

"Mrs Brown, you called for me?" Benedict said as he entered the headteacher's office.

Mrs Brown waved him in as she tapped away at her laptop, finishing up an important email. Benedict headed over to the tea and coffee station Mrs Brown had set up by the window in her office. He made himself a black coffee and prepared a mint and green tea for the headteacher, which he brought over and set beside her. Settling into one chair opposite her desk, Benedict sat quietly, waiting for her to finish.

Mrs Brown picked up her tea gratefully. She took a sip as though it were the first good thing to happen to her that day. Running a hand over her face and hair, she sighed deeply before speaking. "Thank you for coming so quickly. I've been meaning to discuss something with you for a while now; things just got away from me."

"Everything ok?"

"Not really, no. As you are probably aware, the students' mental health is suffering. In addition, the school's reputation is at an all-time high, and as a result, the students are feeling the pressure to perform to the considerable standards set forth by previous students. Look at these," Mrs Brown said, sliding a folder across her desk.

When Benedict opened it, his jaw dropped. The folder was filled with stats from some of the school's best students. Their grades were slipping, attendance in extracurricular activities was down by fifteen percent, and only a handful had applied for the rewards program. A few of the students' attendance was slipping too. According to the notes that accompanied this documentation, the school hadn't seen a dip like this since its founding. The situation was alarming, and it pained Benedict to find out that his students were suffering.

"What can we do?" he asked, already considering several ways he could be more encouraging to the students, should it seem like they needed additional support. Not that any of his students needed it. None of their names were on that list.

"I have a plan, don't you worry. But I am afraid we will lose many investors if word gets out about this, and the students will suffer even more." Mrs Brown settled back in her chair, obviously enjoying the aroma of her tea, which Benedict always found overpowering. She was silent a moment as if considering her words. "Do you remember Charlotte Black?"

The change in topic, quite frankly, surprised him. His mind flashed to his time at the school as a student. He remembered Charlotte. She had left him to do their science fair presentation alone while she swanned off to London on a modelling audition. He could never forget her or the way she turned up at his house and blamed him for taking the credit for a presentation he'd completed without her. He nodded his response.

"Well, she will be here on Monday. She will sit in on several classes, yours included. I've called her in to help the students, but for the first week, she will just be observing. I believe she is the best person to help us get The Northern Swan back to where it needs to be," Mrs Brown said, setting her empty cup on her desk.

He chuckled, thinking this was a joke. "What is she going to teach them? How to accessorize?"

Mrs Brown looked over him with confusion and a slight annoyance. "I take it you two didn't keep in touch? She's an award-winning psychologist now. Studied at Cambridge and is moving back to Fernbrook as we speak," Mrs Brown said.

Benedict stared at her with a blank expression. *Charlotte Black? A psychologist?* Surely, they couldn't be talking about the same person.

"I don't think she needs to sit in on my classes," Benedict finally said. "None of my students are on this list."

Mrs Brown's expression was sombre as she pulled two more folders from her desk drawer. When Benedict scanned the two folders, he found several of his students' names, all from years ten and eleven.

Guilt ran through him. Had he turned into his father? Was he pushing his students too hard? He felt sick. He was failing his students. This was the last thing he wanted to do.

Mrs Brown's smile was sympathetic. "Don't worry about it for now. Once Charlotte has completed her assessment, we will know how to proceed. Enjoy your weekend." Mrs Brown dismissed him.

Chapter Seven

MONDAY ROLLED AROUND QUICKER than Benedict would have liked. He had struggled all weekend to be forced to work with Charlotte again. He spent his Sunday afternoon searching out Charlotte on social media, but all her profiles were set as private, and he didn't much fancy requesting her as a friend just so he could dig further. There was very little information about her modelling career online, but there were a handful of photographs that showed her to be every bit as beautiful as he remembered. He also found a few practices where she had worked and was surprised to see she had done quite well. But, to Benedict, none of that mattered. To him, she would always be the same self-centred little girl who bailed on their science fair presentation. She had likely only become a psychologist for the prestige, somehow hustling her way to the top like she had back when they were in school together.

Benedict always arrived at The Northern Swan earlier than everyone else. He liked to make himself a coffee and read the morning paper in the empty staff room before heading to his classroom to prepare for the day's lessons. When he arrived at the teacher's car park, a silver Audi A3 was the only car in view. He didn't recognise the car and instantly knew it had to belong to Charlotte.

His suspicions were confirmed when he opened the staff room door and found Charlotte making herself a coffee. She had changed little. She still wore her hair loose, down her back, as he remembered her. She was dressed in the highest fashions. A long black calf-length skirt with a white silk Chanel blouse tucked into the waistline seemed better suited for lunch at a fancy restaurant, not for quietly observing a classroom. Her skyscraper tall stilettos Benedict thought were most definitely Christian Louboutin's, identifiable by the famous red bottoms.

She turned to look at him when she heard the door open and smiled, ready to welcome whoever walked through. However, her smile fell when her piercing green eyes landed on Benedict.

"Coffee? How do you take it?" she asked, turning back to the coffee machine.

"I can make my own thanks," he answered, dropping his newspaper on his usual chair and pushing past her to get to the machine.

They didn't speak another word to each other for the next thirty minutes until other teachers arrived. Benedict was happy to have someone else to talk to and was even more delighted when Mrs Brown showed up, and Charlotte left with her.

"Awkward much?" Siobhan Calister, the drama teacher, asked with a grin after they had gone.

"Not at all, I just had nothing to say to her," he answered, folding his paper with what was probably more care than needed. Calister, being a former student, recalled the tension between them, then and now.

"Boys and their childish grudges. It's been what? Fifteen years? Move on already." Siobhan chuckled before grabbing her bag and heading off to the drama room.

"GOOD MORNING, year elevens. How was your weekend?" Benedict asked as he walked into his classroom.

The students lit up and began telling him about everything they had done. They chatted and laughed for a while before Benedict realised Charlotte was sitting at the back of the class. A pair of red cat-eye shaped glasses perched on the end of her nose as she made notes in a large black folder on her lap.

"We have a special guest with us today, class. If you turn to the back, you will see Charlotte Black, another former student of these halls. She is here to observe today," Benedict said trying to put as much enthusiasm as possible into the introduction.

Charlotte shot him an annoyed look before turning towards the students, who all turned to look at her. "Thank you, deputy head Sterling, but please, pretend that I am not here. Carry on as normal." She smiled at the class.

"Don't worry, I intend to," Benedict mumbled under his breath before continuing with his class.

As the day went on, Benedict grew agitated to see Charlotte seemed to make a point of sitting in on all of his classes. She also was spending a great deal of time scribbling notes. He tried to ignore her but couldn't keep his eyes off her and struggled to control his temper when one of his first-year students recognised Charlotte from her modelling days.

"Silence! Eyes front. This is a business class, not the catwalk," Benedict boomed when his class became unruly.

"Sir?" A student raised her hand, waving it enthusiastically.

Benedict nodded for her to continue before taking a seat behind his desk.

"While modelling isn't a traditional career, it still requires you to know and understand business and finance, does it not?" the student asked.

Benedict looked to the back of the room to see Charlotte now sat up straighter trying to hold back a grin and waited patiently for his answer.

"I suppose," Benedict began, not knowing how to answer and not liking how Charlotte seemed to enjoy herself.

"It does indeed. I had to organise my calendar, my taxes, and approach my career as a business venture. A lot of models don't realise how much work goes into it. Everyone assumes it's just posing for pictures, but I assure you, there's a lot going on beneath the surface that people don't realise. Perhaps The Northern Swan should expand their business management curriculum to include modelling," Charlotte said with a smile.

Benedict clenched his jaw and tried to hide his annoyance as several female students cheered and chirped their excitement at the idea.

"I do not think enough students here are interested in modelling to justify a change in curriculum," Benedict said quickly before this could turn into a long discussion destined to derail the remaining minutes of class time.

"Have you asked?" Charlotte asked.

Benedict didn't answer and found a quick way to bypass her question and carry on with his day as usual.

TUESDAY MORNING, Benedict arrived to find Charlotte had once again arrived before him. When he entered the staff room, she was there waiting for him, with her coffee already in hand, a black coffee in his deputy head mug sitting on the table.

"Thank you, you didn't need to do that," he said, taking the coffee and sitting on the sofa by the window.

"I feel like we may have gotten off on the wrong foot yesterday. I apologise for goading the students, I saw an opportunity, and I took it. It made me laugh how the great boy-genius didn't have the answers." She grinned.

Benedict didn't so much as look up from his coffee, "Don't call me that. I always hated that nickname." Charlotte was quiet, and Benedict shot his head up to find her staring intently at him. "And don't psychoanalyse me either."

"I wasn't planning to. I never knew the nickname bothered you so much. I'm sorry. I won't use it again," she said honestly.

"I'm glad you arrived when you did, I'm spending the rest of the week observing the other classes, but I'd like to speak to each teacher individually at the end of the week. Which day works better for you? Friday or Saturday?" she asked, pulling a small leather diary from her Louis Vuitton handbag.

"Excuse me?" Benedict peered at her from over his newspaper.

"I'll be speaking with the students of concern on Thursday, so

Friday and Saturday are the only days I am free," she answered, flicking through the pages.

"Friday is fine. Preferably during school hours," Benedict huffed as he gave up any pretence of reading and dropped the paper on the couch for someone else to read. He left the staff room heading back to his class, still fuming.

CHARLOTTE COULD SENSE that Benedict wasn't happy with her arrival, and while she had grown, she felt he had not. He was still self-absorbed and seemed to think that he was superior to everyone else. While the other teachers welcomed her feedback and were more than happy to help her and let her observe their classes, Benedict seemed to go out of his way to make her job difficult.

He missed their meeting on Friday, and when she turned up the following Monday to ask him about his students, she was lucky if she got more than yes and no answers from him. To her surprise, the students couldn't speak highly enough of him. He was encouraging, thoughtful, and always kept their classes engaging. The students couldn't decide who they liked more of all their teachers, Benedict or Simon.

Maybe he has changed, she thought.

It wasn't until one student asked about the science fair and commented on how he had read somewhere that Charlotte and Benedict were supposed to present the project together, and at *that*, Charlotte realised he still resented her for leaving that day.

Oh please, is he still harbouring anger towards me because of that? He was the one in the wrong after all.

At the end of the month, Charlotte called Mrs Brown and Benedict into the headteacher's office to present her findings. She never expected the month to end the way it had.

"Charlotte, do you have any plans after this?" Mrs Brown asked.

"As in?"

"Job prospects?" Mrs Brown asked.

"Not as yet, why do you ask?"

"From what you have found, I feel like The Northern Swan has failed its students. Not just since my taking over, but in general. What I am about to propose should probably have been done years ago. I feel the students would benefit from having you around. We have enough extra cash in the school budget to hire another full-time staff member. How would you feel about becoming The Northern Swan's new student counsellor?" Mrs Brown beamed.

Chapter Eight

MRS BROWN excitedly introduced Charlotte as the inaugural school counsellor at the next school assembly. The students seemed happy to have someone they could talk to about their concerns. Mrs Brown had given Charlotte an office just off the main hallway. It was an old classroom that, as the school grew, became too small to house the students and had sat unused for years. Charlotte knew that she would have her work cut out for her, but she never expected so many students to come seek her advice so quickly.

Most of the students' concerns, which was expected, was that there was too much pressure to perform to such high standards. She was surprised to see how many students seemed to felt that pressure more from their parents than from the school.

By far, the easier problem to solve had been the issues concerning the rewards program. She could quickly dispel many concerns the students felt about the program. And both Benedict and Mrs Brown were ecstatic to receive more applications. The idea of more students feeling hopeful towards their future was just the pick-me-up that the teachers all needed.

Within the first few months, everyone had seen a turnaround. The students were happier, productivity had improved, and the students felt a lot more comfortable discussing issues, which were quickly addressed. In addition, Charlotte's new role had proven to be a huge success and even caught the attention of the local newspaper, which was quite happy to sing her praises.

"Thank you so much, Miss Black. You're the greatest," beamed a first-year student as she left Charlotte's new office.

"You're welcome, sweetie. My door is always open if you need to talk," Charlotte called as the young girl ran off to her next lesson.

The main cause for concern, that the students were feeling too much pressure, was being addressed. New school slogans and parent/student handbooks were being developed to promote the importance of achieving a work/life balance. However, Charlotte found she was still inundated with students who wanted to talk about everything and everything. Problems at home, issues with other students, exams, college and university applications, driving lessons. The list was endless. But wasn't that why Charlotte had taken the job in the first place? She remembered having similar concerns and wished that she would have had someone she could have turned to when she was a student there. Perhaps she would still have a relationship with her mother if she did.

"Someone seems busy," Benedict said with a smile, as he handed Charlotte a latte from the staff room one morning. She'd been there several weeks now.

"Thanks, you have no idea how much I needed this," Charlotte said gratefully, accepting the coffee and taking a long sip.

"The students love you," Benedict said as he spotted several students hovering outside her door.

"I know. I love them too. It feels right being back here, you know?" she asked, waving the next student in, telling him she would be with him in just a moment.

"You are doing great work here. I feel like I owe you an apology," he said, shifting his cup awkwardly in his hands.

"Really? Why?" Charlotte asked, eyeing him over the rim of her glasses.

"Don't make me say it," he said nervously, rubbing the back of his neck.

"Whatever do you mean?" Charlotte teased, offering Benedict a wink.

He seemed startled by the flirtation, but Charlotte ignored it. She thanked him again for the coffee and excused herself so she could get back to her students.

BENEDICT WALKED BACK to his office in a daze. He couldn't understand why the innocent wink from Charlotte had him feeling the way it did. He had butterflies in his stomach. And seriously, was he *blushing*?

The longer he worked with Charlotte, the more he found he was softening to her. He wondered if perhaps he had misjudged her. She often worked way past school hours to help students work through their issues. The kids loved her, and so did the rest of the staff.

She was brighter than he remembered, or perhaps he had never paid that much attention to her. Just because she took pride in her appearance, didn't mean she was self-absorbed or obsessed with her looks. And she was very much a hard worker. She was beautiful enough that she could easily have continued with her modelling career. Why hadn't she continued? What had changed?

As he got to his office. He suddenly realised how, lately, she was occupying quite a bit of his attention. The mere thought of her had slowly made him smile. He wasn't sure how he felt about that.

What's wrong with me?

Chapter Nine

"HEY, what's up with Benedict? He normally arrives at the same time as I do, but lately, he seems.... I don't know, distant?" Charlotte asked Simon and Siobhan as she sat with them in the staff room.

"It's getting to that time of year again. He always stresses out when the science fair is around the corner," Simon said, absentmindedly stirring his tea.

Charlotte stiffened a little. Surely, their science fair project had had little impact that it still affected him?

"What do you mean?" she asked, carefully keeping the question casual and light.

"Well, every year since The Northern Swan first won, we have taken the prize home again. Since joining the school as a previous winner, the students have always sought him to help with their projects. The competition was tough when you guys competed, but it's even worse now. Poor guy works on every student project with them, to not show any favouritism," Siobhan answered.

Charlotte gasped. "Every student? Last I heard, The Northern Swan enters at least twelve projects in the science fair."

"Yup, every single one. I'm surprised the poor guy gets any sleep,"

Siobhan said, pointing out the window as Benedict got out of his beat-up car.

His hair was messy, his jawline could do with a shave, and his tie was off centre. He had deep bags under his eyes and looked like a man with the world's weight on his shoulders.

Charlotte stood and headed round to the door leading to the car park. As she opened the door, she witnessed several students running to Benedict and hounding him with questions before they all scurried off. He struggled with his bags and dropped several books, cursing to himself, running his hands through his hair, and messing it up even further.

Charlotte hadn't noticed how good-looking he was before. And it warmed her heart a little to see he put his students before himself. She strode over to him and knelt to help him retrieve his books.

"Let me give you a hand with that." She smiled as she picked up the last book and handed it to him.

"Thanks." Benedict yawned.

"When was the last time you got any sleep?" she asked, and without thinking, reached out to fix his tie. Her heart skipped a beat as his eyes fell on her.

His breath caught in his throat at her touch. "Thank you," was all Benedict could muster.

"I hear you have been helping the students with their science projects. Need a hand? It must be hard juggling twelve projects and your lesson plans while still helping to run the school," Charlotte said coyly.

Charlotte noticed Benedict tense at the offer of her help, but she didn't know what to say or do to make him relax.

"It's fine. I've helped them for the near ten years I've been at this school.... but thanks for the offer," he said, finally offering her a smile.

"Well, you know where I am if you need a helping hand."

They walked back into the school in silence, but oddly enough, it wasn't an awkward silence.

"The students know you helped with the win that year. Every student I have worked with has been told that it was a team effort. I make sure that they know."

Charlotte froze in her tracks. "Really? Why?" she asked.

"Because it *was* a team effort," he answered.

Charlotte could tell he wanted to say more but was too afraid. As she looked up at him, her head cocked to the side, her green eyes locked on his pale blue ones. A thought occurred to her. Benedict still battled with the issues of his father. He was still that scared, unloved five-year-old wanting the approval of others. It broke her heart a little. She found she wanted to talk to him about it. But from what she knew of Benedict, she knew he wouldn't take her interference well.

Maybe it's best to let him come to me, she thought.

Chapter Ten

CHARLOTTE WATCHED, over the next two months, as Benedict stretched himself thin to help all the students prepare for the science fair. He tried to act like he was coping well, but Charlotte had walked past his office and classrooms a few times and noticed him asleep at his desk. She had taken to sneaking in with a coffee and leaving it for when he woke up, which, on inspection, was not long after the aroma hit his nose.

The day before the science fair, Mrs Brown called Benedict and Charlotte into her office.

"This is going to be quite an experience for the kids this year. So I thought it might be a good idea for Charlotte to accompany you to the fair," the headmistress said, her eyes dancing between the two, looking for any potential conflict.

"I'd be more than happy to help," Charlotte answered.

"That's if she actually turns up this time," Benedict mumbled before he yawned loudly.

"I heard that," Charlotte said dryly.

"I was joking. I'd be happy for you to help...and thanks for all the coffee," he said, keeping his eyes anywhere but on Charlotte.

She smiled and blushed a little that he had noticed she had been the one to bring him his liquid energy.

"Wonderful," Mrs Brown cheered.

The next day, Benedict and Charlotte met the students in the schoolyard, organised them, helped them pack their experiments into their parents' cars, dished out the itinerary for the day, and handed out directions.

"Want to drive up separately or together?" Benedict asked.

"Oh...I don't mind either way," Charlotte said, a little taken back.

"My car isn't as nice as yours, but feel free to hop in," he said with a soft smile.

Charlotte's hands trembled. She quickly climbed into his car and settled in for the forty-minute journey to the fair.

"Excited about today?" she asked.

"More ready for it to be over. While it's fun, it's taking its toll. I used to love the fair, now I dread it," he answered, startling Charlotte with his honesty.

"I did offer to help," she said.

"I know, I'm just.... well.... I guess.... yeah," he stuttered, causing them both to chuckle.

"Do you think we have a shot at winning this year?" she asked. She hadn't reviewed the entrants for the fair, so she was excited to be viewing the fair with fresh eyes.

"We better. I've worked non-stop to make sure the kids are ready. You already know the kids have stressed themselves out way too much over it."

"Well, I'm here to help now." She smiled.

The car journey was silent for a while, Benedict keeping his eyes on the road and following the school bus carrying the other students who observed and offer encouragement, along with the rest of the staff. Charlotte stared out the window, thinking of all the things she wanted to ask but couldn't.

"I never apologised to you, did I?" Benedict asked, breaking their silence.

"For what?"

"Taking all the credit for our project. But, let's face it, it's been the elephant in the room since you joined the school. And I think I have harboured ill feelings towards you for too long," Benedict answered, surprising her for the second time that day.

In shock, Charlotte turned, her neck making an audible click at that speed.

"You did? I never noticed," she smiled, winking at him when he glanced her way. "It's in the past. Let's just leave it at that and enjoy today."

They pulled up at the hotel hosting the fair. Charlotte stopped Benedict, gently grabbing his arm as he tried to leave the car. "I'm sorry too for leaving you that day. I know you had issues with public speaking back then."

"Thanks," Benedict said, his eyes not leaving her perfectly manicured hand on his arm.

They entered the madness of the science fair, and Charlotte was right on hand when the students showed pre-show jitters. She couldn't help but notice how Benedict had jumped straight into superhero mode, helping when one student broke down when her project wouldn't work. He pulled out his tools and helped her fix things in no time.

"Welcome to this year's science fair. So, who will take home the prize this year? Will The Northern Swan school from the Lake District keep the crown? Or will someone take it from them? Let's find out, shall we? Sooooo, let the science fair begin!" boomed the commentator's voice as everyone cheered.

As the judges made their rounds and Charlotte took in the vast space filled with parents, students, and faculty, she felt a pang of guilt that she left Benedict to do it all alone fifteen years ago. Even she had to admit that the fair was overwhelming.

"So...it means.... um...." A student stuttered, presentation nerves kicking in. Charlotte felt for her as the young girl's eyes filled with tears.

"It means we can reduce..." Benedict prompted, putting a supportive hand on the young girl's shoulder.

"It means we can reduce plastic waste and save money on creating biodegradable materials so that if they end up in the ocean or landfills, wildlife won't suffer when they eat it. Therefore, no longer contaminating the food chain." The girl flashed him a smile as she spoke, triumphant now that she was remembering her lines.

The support from her teacher seemed just the ticket, as she continued to explain how her materials would be a superior alternative to plastic and how they could also help grow and maintain the growth of deforested areas.

"Very impressive, Laney. We are impressed," said one judge.

"Thank you, Sir," Laney said, flinging her arms around Benedict in a hug, who looked taken back by the sudden show of affection.

"That's what teachers are for. I knew you could do it. I feared public speaking once too," he reassured her, gently peeling himself away.

It warmed Charlotte's heart to see how Benedict had an extra spring in his step after that. However, it also confirmed her previous thoughts that he just wanted love and approval. *His father really did a number on him,* she thought.

"What?" Benedict asked when he realised Charlotte was staring at him.

"Oh.... nothing," Charlotte stuttered, looking away.

She noticed a twinkle in his eyes being with the kids, and science seemed to thrive. She watched him for the rest of the day, battling with herself, wondering why she couldn't stop smiling at him. It was hard for her not to notice the lingering looks he shot her way too.

The Northern Swan won first prize again that year, no surprise to anyone. The regional news and local, newspapers came at the winning student with notepads and flashing cameras. They clustered to interview the successful student.

"I couldn't have done it without the help and guidance of Mr Sterling and Miss Black."

"Let's get a picture with them, shall we?" asked the reporters.

Benedict and Charlotte stood on either side of the school's winner until the reporters told them to get closer. A step closer, Benedict hooked his arm around the small of Charlotte's back, and she straightened, trying to ignore the electricity shooting through her at his touch. Instead, she stretched her arm around his waist and smiled a little brighter at the feeling of him reacting under her touch.

"So tell us, Mr Sterling, years after your win, how does it feel that one of your students has taken the crown?" asked the reporter.

"Well, I can't take all the credit. My win back then wasn't truly my win. It was mine and Miss Black's here. It was unfortunate on the day that she couldn't make it, and I was a pig-headed student who took all the credit. But, without her, The Northern Swan wouldn't have the success it does today," Benedict smiled at Charlotte.

She couldn't believe he had finally given her the credit she deserved, and she felt her eyes tear up. She mouthed thank you, and he surprised her, offering her a wink as they continued the interviews.

Back at school, Mrs Brown and the rest of the staff celebrated with the students and their parents before sending them all home.

"I hear he finally admitted you helped with the project," Siobhan said as she nudged Charlotte with her elbow.

"Do I detect a spark? He has definitely softened up since you arrived."

Charlotte looked over to Benedict as Siobhan walked away. Charlotte blushed when she noticed he was looking her way. He joined her at the awards cabinet.

"Are you coming to Lake House on Saturday to celebrate the end of the year with the other teachers?" he asked.

With a slight smile, but keeping her eyes on the trophies and ribbons, she replied, "Sure. Will you be there?"

"I might be. I haven't decided yet," he answered before sliding off to re-join Simon and the others.

Siobhan's words swam in Charlotte's mind. *Was there a spark?* She had to admit that he was attractive. And she had felt a jolt of electricity when he hooked his arm around her for the pictures. Would she say anything to him? Did he feel the same? *I guess we can explore further on Saturday;* she thought.

Chapter Eleven

THE TEACHERS WOULD GATHER at The Lake House at the end of every school year. The Lake House was a local favourite, having started out as a traditional English pub near the lake in West Water. Over the years, it had been expanded to accommodate Fernbrook's growing popularity. It boasted a large open bar area separated into sections. The left of the main bar area was dedicated to pub games. It housed a pool table and a dartboard and had a beautiful view of the lake from the large bay windows that filled the wall. The other side was set out into booths for small gatherings with a jukebox in the corner next to an outdated cigarette machine, which was now only used for display purposes. The central area was set up for dining as The Lake House served food around the clock. At the back of the main bar was a door leading to the basement's function room. This spacious, inviting room was mainly used for private parties. It was here that The Northern Swan teachers had a permanent booking at the end of every school year.

The function room had its own bar, a private buffet of prepared food, and an impressive dance floor space. The stage area was set up for a DJ or a live band. The teachers always hired the same DJ. DJ Mike - no pun intended, as he was the only DJ in the area to offer karaoke as part of his booking.

Saturday arrived, and Charlotte felt a little nervous about the gathering. She couldn't determine if it was because Benedict had hinted that he would be there. When he asked her if she was going, she had a feeling he implied he wanted her to be there. She was sure that she had felt something between them over the last few weeks, but at the same time, she wondered if she was just imagining it?

"For crying out loud, you are a grown-ass woman. Not a child," she said to her reflection in the mirror as she tried on yet another dress, trying to find the perfect look in case he was there after all.

After emptying her wardrobe, she settled on a black and red floral dress. It was tasteful and hugged her curves but was still casual enough that if Benedict didn't feel the way he appeared, it would look like she hadn't made too much effort. Then, sliding her feet into her 'lucky' black Louboutin's, she applied a light layer of red lipstick and fluffed her hair. She had agreed to meet the girls for a round of drinks in the bar first because, as Siobhan said, "The guys are always late."

"Girl, you look hot! Trying to impress a certain deputy head teacher, are we?" Siobhan said with a whistle that turned all heads towards Charlotte as she entered the bar.

"This old thing? I'm sure I've worn it to work a few times," she lied as she stepped in to hug her colleagues.

"I'd remember you in that. What is it?" Siobhan asked.

Charlotte always felt uncomfortable when Siobhan commented on her clothes or the relationship, however non-existent, between her and Benedict. Although Siobhan had always been a loud person and appeared to have no filter or awareness of people's boundaries, that day, she seemed loud. Charlotte assumed the half-finished Bottlenose wine over her shoulder had something to do with it, and suddenly her excitement for the night wavered.

"Oh, it's Prada," Charlotte answered, squeezing past and ordering a brandy on the rocks from the bar.

"Wow! She dresses sharp and drinks sharply too. We will have to watch this one, ladies," Siobhan said gaily, waving her hand expansively as she spoke. Wine came near to escaping her glass with the movement, and Charlotte cringed.

"Oh pipe down, girl, the rate you're going, it's *you* we will all need to keep an eye on," Mrs Brown groaned. "Don't mind her. She's a loud-mouth at the best of times. She's even worse after a few glasses of wine."

"She is harmless, really." Charlotte smiled back to show there was no harm done.

"She's right about one thing, you look beautiful."

"Thanks....so what's the plan for the evening?" Charlotte asked, trying to gear the conversation onto the subject she really wanted to talk about – whether or not Benedict was coming.

"Us girls have a few drinks and wait for the guys to arrive, then we head down to the function room and party the night away," Mrs Brown said, raising her glass of white wine in a mock toast to the evening ahead.

"I never knew this was a thing the teachers did. Does everyone come?"

"It's a fairly new tradition. I started it when I joined the school. All the staff usually attend.... well, apart from Benedict. He isn't normally the party animal type," Mrs Brown offered.

"Oh, how sad! He has worked so hard this year. I should think he could use a break," Charlotte said, trying to hide her disappointment.

A part of her had hoped he would come, and it vexed her she couldn't place why. As the girls continued to drink and the guys slowly arrived, Charlotte began planning her escape, especially since there was no sign of Benedict.

Charlotte was just thinking about how she could slip away without notice when her train of thought was interrupted by Siobhan yelling in her ear. At first, she wasn't sure she heard correctly over the noise of Simon drunkenly singing a Queen classic on karaoke.

"I guess you made an impression. He never shows up to these things."

Charlotte looked over to the door as Benedict walked in. Her breath caught in her throat at the sight of him. He wasn't in his usual worn-out suits and vest he wore for school. Instead, he wore dark jeans and a fitted black cotton shirt. From the audible collective gasp from the other female staff Charlotte was surrounded by, she could tell his trim physique wasn't lost on them either.

"Well, look who cleans up well. Those suits don't do him any justice," Siobhan slurred into Charlotte's ear.

Benedict scanned the room, and his eyes locked with Charlotte's. His blank expression softened, and he gave her a slight grin as he walked over.

"You came," was all Charlotte could muster by way of greeting.

"As did you. Fancy a drink?" he asked, offering her his hand.

Siobhan and the girls let off a chorus of 'oohs' mockingly as Charlotte took his hand and followed him to the first-floor bar.

"Sorry, I had to get you away from them. Siobhan has a reputation for being a sloppy drunk, and I can't tolerate it," he said.

Charlotte didn't know what to say. Her stomach gave a flip at the touch of his hand, but her heartfelt disappointment at his reply tempered this.

Easy girl. This means nothing. "I understand," Charlotte said, giving a smile of commiseration.

"Besides, it's easier to talk by the bar, a bit quieter. But, man, is Simon killing that song. It's a classic. I feel like crying. It's a crime against music," he said. They listened as they heard the intro music and the DJ setting up downstairs.

"Don't be mean; he's trying his best!" she teased. "Or do you think you can do a better job?"

"Oh, I know I can," he said, his eyes flashing, sending a thrill through Charlotte.

"That I would like to see," she chuckled as she ordered their drinks.

"Keep plying me with the good stuff, and you might."

They waited in companionable silence as the bartender poured their drinks. Ben smiled as he sipped his whiskey. "You look beautiful, by the way," he said, noticeably keeping his eyes from meeting hers.

"This old thing? .... you clean up pretty well yourself. Who would have known there was such a body under those suits," Charlotte responded, shocking herself and Benedict with her daring attempt at flirtation.

Maybe starting drinking so early was a bad idea, she thought, setting her glass back on the bar before she could make matters any more awkward.

They made small talk and discussed the kids and the rewards program for the rest of the evening. Neither of them really delved into anything too deep or personal, yet the conversation flowed as freely as the water in the surrounding lake and never felt awkward. Charlotte was pleasantly surprised at how at ease she felt around him. Or was it the brandy? She didn't care. She was having more fun than she realised.

"Come on, love birds, come dance with us," Mrs Brown yelled, grabbing their hands, and dragging them to the dance floor.

As they awkwardly danced with each other and the rest of their team, they both shared the odd glance whenever someone else commented on the apparent spark between them. If others noticed it, surely it wasn't just imagination.

Charlotte grinned as the DJ asked for any more song requests. "Go on then." She nudged Benedict in a friendly way with a nod towards where the karaoke was set up.

"What? I was joking!" Benedict played at being panicked, looking around wildly for escape in over-exaggerated horror.

"Tease," she poked him in the ribs, making him laugh. Obviously, he was ticklish.

"I will if you will," he grinned, grabbing her hand, and dragging her to the stage.

Charlotte tried to pull away, but his grip was like iron. "Oh god, no. I don't sing. Not in front of people anyway," she protested.

"Oh, come on, everyone is so drunk, no one will remember in the morning," he said with a wink as he scooped her up around the waist and planted her squarely down in front of the lyric screen.

Charlotte looked out over the room, and her heart raced. Stage fright was real. Benedict handed her a microphone, and one look into his eyes was all it took to make her nerves melt away. The first notes to Sonny and Cher's "Don't Go Breaking My Heart" began. To the amazement of Charlotte and everyone else in the room, Benedict could sing.

Chapter Twelve

MONDAY MORNING ARRIVED, and with it, the last week of the school year. All the coursework was wrapped up for the year, so most classes were calm, and some teachers even allowed students to just relax and watch movies.

In the staff room Monday morning, Charlotte prepared for her last few appointments with the graduating students before they left for college and university. She couldn't help but notice how Benedict was absent. She hoped he was ok as she sat stirring her coffee, remembering Saturday night. After their karaoke duet, they'd danced the night away with the rest of the team before her feet hurt so much that she had to sit down. Thinking back, she honestly couldn't remember when Benedict left. She remembered one minute he was there and the next he wasn't. They had shared a moment without a doubt, but something still held them back.

"Morning," Benedict's voice brought her head up quickly. For a moment, it felt as though she'd summoned him somehow with her thoughts.

"Hey, how was your Sunday?" she asked, smiling as he came into the room.

"Ok, nothing much to write home about. Yours?"

"Oh, I was suffering after Saturday. I don't think I will ever drink like that again," Charlotte chuckled.

Benedict grinned slightly, but his smile faded quickly as he turned away to make his morning coffee. He seemed distracted. Without so much as another word or even a glance in Charlotte's direction, he grabbed his coffee and headed to his classroom.

Charlotte stared after him, wondering what she'd said wrong. She reminded herself it would be half an hour before the students were due to arrive, and everyone knew Benedict enjoyed spending the last weeks helping his final year students with their plans and with the winners from the awards program. He probably had work to do.

"Huh, I guess that spark was just the whiskey," Siobhan said over her shoulder as she too left the room.

"Yeah, I guess you are right," Charlotte mumbled, thankful no one else was there to notice the snub.

BENEDICT SEEMED to avoid Charlotte at every opportunity. He stopped taking his coffee in the staff room and even shut himself in his office at lunch to avoid seeing her. She worried she had offended him. She wanted to ask what she had done wrong, but her pride wouldn't let her. By the last day of school, the infatuation began to fade as she convinced herself it was all in her head. She finished her last appointment and left at lunch.

She didn't need any awkward or false goodbyes.

"WHERE IS CHARLOTTE?" Simon asked as the teachers all gathered in the car park to lock up for the summer.

"She left at lunch. She finished her last appointment and went home. No need for her to stick around," Mrs Brown said.

"Do you think she is embarrassed about Saturday?" Siobhan asked.

"Why should she be embarrassed? She wasn't the one who needed three of us to put her in a taxi after throwing up all over herself," Benedict said, shocking Siobhan and the rest of the staff.

Sliding into his car, he didn't give anyone a second look before leaving, happy to start his summer alone. While most of the teachers had holidays abroad planned or family trips, Benedict was happy with his DIY gardening and reading.

Why did I spend the week avoiding her? A lot can happen over one summer. If she meets someone else, it's my fault. I should have made my move.

Benedict cursed himself as he drove back to his childhood home.

Chapter Thirteen

BENEDICT SPENT the first few weeks of the summer holidays trying not to think about Charlotte. But everywhere he looked, he saw something that would remind him of her. It was even worse when he found out Simon had videoed their performance on the teacher's night out and uploaded it to Facebook. Benedict rewatched it so many times he felt embarrassed and was glad no one but him knew how often he'd hit 'replay.'

To busy himself, he took his father's old boat out on the lake and occupied himself with repairs—albeit unnecessary repairs—around his home. He also finished reading the latest deceptive comics, which was obviously a lot quicker than he would have liked. Then, as the new academic year approached, he kept himself busy with new lesson plans until he was fresh out of things to do.

Rewatching the karaoke video, he noticed Charlotte had commented.

Simon, I'm going to kill you. Lol. Take it down. I look ridiculous.

After staring at his phone for way too long, he replied to her comment:

Don't you dare take it down! It's a great video of a great night.

Not long after, Charlotte sent him a friend request, and without hesitation, he accepted. He spent the rest of his evening scanning through her pictures and posts. She didn't post too often, but he noticed she'd spent two weeks in Italy with friends. From what he could see, it looked like she'd had a great time. He hoped she would start a chat as he found he was too nervous to start the conversation himself.

What is wrong with me? We had one night out together with colleagues, and now I can't stop thinking about her.

He hated how he questioned himself. What was wrong with being interested? The more he looked through her social media, the more he learned about Charlotte. She shared interesting articles about the world and had pinned the article that pictured them to the top of her feed with the caption, 'Very Proud.' Her words rang in his mind, "You clean up pretty well yourself. Who would have known there was such a body under those suits?" The picture did make them look pretty good. Not perfect, mind you, but good.

He made a mental note to go back to the gym.

Scrolling through her photos, he lost track of time and didn't know precisely when he drifted off to sleep, but he awoke the following day with his phone on the floor.

The last week before the fall semester was due to begin, Benedict hit the gym first thing every morning and emptied his fridge and cupboards of all junk food. *Damn, how much junk do I eat?* He asked himself when he realised how empty his kitchen now was. *I will go to the supermarket tomorrow.*

With the weekend almost over, Benedict realised just how much work he still had left to do before work would resume and lost track of time preparing new lesson plans for his students due to start year eleven. When he finally looked up, he noticed he had spent the entire day at his computer, and the stores were due to close soon. Hurriedly, he changed into jeans and a white shirt and drove to the all-night supermarket just outside of Fernbrook.

Satisfied with his now full and healthy shopping trolly, he paid the cashier and thanked the girl for packing his bags. Then, while putting his groceries in the car's boot, he heard a woman's startled scream for help. Immediately, he abandoned the task and jogged around to the other side of the car park to see what was wrong and if he could somehow be of assistance.

His heart stopped, and his blood boiled as he saw Charlotte's Audi A3. It was well into the evening, and the car park had little light, but another cry for help pinpointed her location. She was struggling to fight off a tall, rangy man who was trying to take her handbag from her. The thief grabbed at her arm, and Charlotte looked terrified.

"Hey! Get off her!" Benedict yelled and was on the man in an instant. Furious, he punched the man in the jaw.

The robber dropped to the floor like a bag of potatoes, grabbing his bruised jawline. He jumped to his feet, ready to stand and fight back until he saw the look of thunder Benedict shot his way.

"This is none of your business, buddy," the man snarled.

Benedict grabbed him by the collar and pulled him up, so their faces practically touched. The robber wasn't too much shorter than Benedict, but with the way Benedict was holding him, his toes barely touched the floor.

"Run! Fast and far before I call the police. And if I see you here again, you will get more than this, *buddy*!" Benedict snarled, shoving the guy hard, causing him to stumble and trip over his own feet.

The fear in the man's eyes had no effect on Benedict as he jumped up, shouting an offensive at Charlotte before running off into the night. Benedict turned to help Charlotte pick up her bag. She'd fought hard to keep her belongings, but the shoulder strap had been snapped in the struggle.

"Are you ok?" he asked, helping her up from the ground.

Her usual glowing face was ghostly white in the dim light of the car park, and her eyes glistened as she fought back the tears. Her body trembled under his fingers. Instinctively, he pulled her in and wrapped his arms around her. He cradled her against his chest, hoping she felt safe. She wrapped her arms around him and clung tightly to his shirt as she sobbed. It pained Benedict to see her that way.

"I'm so sorry, I've got makeup all over your shirt," she said when she finally pulled herself away.

She looked up at him, wiping at her eyes, mascara smudged and running in tracks down her face. She still looked so beautiful.

Benedict tucked a stray hair behind her ear and smiled at her. "It will wash out. Come on, let me drive you home," he said, wrapping his arm around her and walking her away from her car.

"But my car..." she protested.

"Do you have any perishable items in your car?"

"I never got a chance to go shopping. He grabbed me as I arrived," she said, her voice cracking again.

"Then I shall bring your car over to your place tomorrow. You can't drive in this state, and it'll be safe enough here," he insisted.

He walked to the store the following morning in true gentleman form, with Charlotte's car keys in hand. When he dropped her off at home the night before, he'd noted what she needed and picked up a few items from the supermarket before driving her car back to her place. He knocked, but she didn't answer. He worried but figured she was probably still sleeping. So, he left the shopping on the doorstep and poked her car keys through her letterbox.

When he arrived home, he found a Facebook message from Charlotte waiting for him.

Sorry I missed you. I slept little last night, so I was still in bed when you called. Thank you for collecting my car and thank you for the shopping, how much do I owe you? P.S. The flowers are beautiful. - C

He quickly typed his reply:

Don't worry about it. I'm just glad I was there to help. If you need anything else, let me know. - B

Thankful she had his number to call if she needed him, he went about his day with a newfound spring in his step. He was never one for confrontation but was glad he'd played the hero.

Chapter Fourteen

CHARLOTTE WOKE up the day school was due to start and felt too scared to leave her house for the first time in her life. She had hardly slept since the incident, even though her better judgement told her she would be fine. Her mind just wouldn't let her leave the safety of her own home.

Logically speaking, she knew it was safe. With all the windows and doors locked, no one could hurt her. She called Mrs Brown but felt too embarrassed to admit she feared leaving her home, so she made her excuses and said she would be back as soon as possible and that she would keep her updated. Feeling a little more at ease now, she didn't have to go to work; she curled up in bed and tried to get some much-needed sleep.

BENEDICT worried when he didn't see her car in the car park, but he figured she might need an extra day to calm down, given her weekend. She had his number and knew she could contact him if needed, so he tried not to worry. As the day passed, he found he made many excuses to walk past her office in hopes the light would be on, and she would be inside. By the time Monday rolled around again, panic had set in. He had messaged her to see if she needed anything, but the message was left unread.

"I bet she has swanned off on another modelling gig. She definitely can't afford her lifestyle on her salary," Siobhan scoffed one morning.

"I doubt it. She sounded pretty bad when I last spoke to her," Mrs Brown offered.

Benedict pulled himself away from his paper, his heart pounding. He should have checked on her and kicked himself for not stopping by after work when she hadn't returned his calls.

"When did you last speak with her?" he asked, a sick feeling coming into the pit of his stomach.

"Two days ago. I haven't been able to get a hold of her since. To be honest, I'm a little worried," Mrs Brown said, filling her teacup for the third time that day.

"She's probably been partying and is nursing a hangover. She's weak if you ask me," Siobhan laughed.

Benedict looked around the staff room and noticed the jury was split. Some seemed to agree with Siobhan. She had always been one to cause trouble and loved starting rumours at school. Her antics had gotten her in a spot of trouble a few times. She was almost expelled because of it once back when they were kids. The other half of the teachers, like himself and Mrs Brown, were used to Siobhan and her wicked tongue. He was glad to see they took no interest in her opinion.

"Not that it's any of your business, but she was almost robbed the weekend before term started," Benedict snapped, folding his paper with such frustration that he tore a few pages.

"What? How do you know?" Mrs Brown asked, her eyes going wide in alarm.

"I was coming out of the supermarket and heard a scream. I followed it, and some jerk was trying to take her handbag. I stopped him, but she was pretty shaken." He shook his head at the memory. "She's a better woman than most and what she does for these students is remarkable. She deserves nothing but your respect, not juvenile claims, or slanderous remarks of her character," Benedict answered, aiming the last of his speech at Siobhan.

Siobhan gasped. "Excuse me?" She never could get her head around it when people called her on her ill behaviour.

"Benedict is right. Any more of that, Siobhan, and you and I will have issues. I will call her again later and check in on her. Poor girl," Mrs Brown said.

"Don't worry, I'll check on her. I doubt she will appreciate the fact that I told you all what happened. I'd rather her hear it from me than thinking everyone was gossiping about her," he said.

As he left school, Caroline, the physical education teacher, ran over carrying a gift basket.

"Here, tell her it's from her work family. It's nothing much. We just want to do what we can to make her feel better," she smiled.

When Benedict inspected the basket further, he found everything from chocolates, an attack alarm, wine, fruit, magazines, and books. Some teachers had given her bath salts, face masks, and other goodies he knew she would love. There was also a card he assumed all the staff had signed, but he knew better than to read it himself.

CHARLOTTE WRAPPED the blanket around her tighter when she heard the knock at the door. Her heart raced, and she developed a cold sweat. *Has he found me?* She panicked. Like a frightened child, she climbed out of bed and curled up in a ball on the floor.

"Charlotte, it's Benedict," she heard him yell through the letterbox.

A sudden calm washed over her, and she made her way downstairs. She didn't care that she was in two-day-old PJs or had mascara rings around her eyes and a bird's nest of hair scrunched up into a messy bun on the top of her head. Slowly she opened the door and allowed him to come inside. He still wore the brown suit, which was at least two sizes too big, and his tie was the usual off-centre mess, but his face was warm and welcoming. She was happier than expected to see him.

"I've missed you at school.... we have all missed you, I mean. Here, this is from the other teachers. I'm sorry. I told them what happened. I know I shouldn't have, but everyone was worried when you hadn't been in touch." Benedict clamped his mouth shut when he realised he was rambling nervously.

"Thank you," she whispered, taking the basket from him, and leading him to the living room. "Would you like a drink?"

"Sit, let me do it," Benedict said, helping her to sit on the sofa and showing himself to the kitchen.

Charlotte sat examining her brown and chipped nails, suddenly self-conscious of her appearance and the mess that was her home now that Benedict was inside. She could hear him searching through cupboards for cups and sugar for coffee and used the time to scurry around the living room, tidying what mess she could.

"Do you have decaf?" he asked, popping his head around the door.

She froze as she straightened some cushions and looked up at his amused face. Her heart fluttered as his smile touched his eyes, and they sparkled back at her.

"What are you doing?" he asked

"Erm...just...cleaning,"

He chuckled. "Why?"

"You're a guest in my home. I don't want you thinking I normally live in a mess like this," she answered honestly.

"Relax, Char, it's fine. You should see my place. Decaf?" He chuckled before heading back in to finish the drinks.

"Top left above the kettle," she yelled after him.

He returned with two coffees and sat opposite her in the chair next to the sofa.

He took off his blazer as he settled himself. "Stupid question, but how are you?" he asked, his eyes soft and caring.

Charlotte's breath caught in her throat as she stared back at the fitted shirt usually hidden by his oversized blazer. He had clearly been working out. The white cotton material barely contained his muscles.

"Sorry." She blushed when she realised she had been wordlessly gawping at him for too long. "I'm okay, I guess," she offered.

He moved to join her on the sofa and gently took her hand in his. Her eyes locked on their combined hands. His hands were rough like he had been doing a lot of work with them recently. She liked how his thumb felt as it stroked the top of her hand.

"Char, it's me. You can tell me," he said, his voice softer than she had ever heard it.

"I've been too scared to leave the house," she admitted.

It was a relief to say the words out loud, but that didn't stop the sting of embarrassment that kept her from looking back at him. Finally, he tucked a finger under her chin and brought her gaze up to his. She hoped he could not feel her trembling.

"It's okay to be scared, but it was a random attack by some low-life. You will never see him again."

She tried to smile. "It's not that big of a town," she reminded him.

"Okay, say he bumps into you again. I will not let anything happen to you." He breathed the words softly, making them a vow while giving her a gentle smile he hoped was reassuring.

"Why?" she asked without thinking.

"Why what?" he asked, letting go of her and sitting straighter. She watched as his invisible walls flew back up, sealing the gentle caring side of Benedict behind an iron wall.

"Why do you care so much?" she asked, hoping, praying for a spark of hope.

"Because..." he trailed off, unable to answer her question.

"It wasn't a random attack," she finally said, taking her coffee from the table and sitting back, away from him.

"What do you mean?" he asked, his brow furrowing towards his nose.

"He was an acquaintance of my mother's. When I told him where to go, he lashed out. That's why I have been so scared. What if he knows where I live?" she asked.

He didn't even have to think about it. "I have a spare room. Or I could sleep on your sofa. But at the end of the day, that would only be a temporary solution. Have you called the police? If you know who he is, they can arrest him," he said.

"I don't know him, she does. It's a long story, and to be honest, I don't really want to talk about it," she sighed.

Benedict nodded, and she was grateful that he respected her wish and didn't press further. It was hard enough to admit to herself, especially since she thought she had left behind that part of her life.

"I'll leave you be, but Char, please promise me something?" he asked, standing up and collecting his blazer. "If you feel unsafe, if you see a shadow or hear a noise that frightens you, please call me. Don't suffer alone," he said.

His words startled her, and it was all she could do to nod her agreement.

Chapter Fifteen

"So sorry to hear about what happened, pet. If you need anything, my door is always open," Simon said.

"Thanks, Si. I'm alright now. Just needed to get my head back in the game," Charlotte responded.

Benedict was happy to see that Charlotte was back at school. She smiled at everyone and seemed like the usual Charlotte to the others. But Benedict noticed the subtle details showing that she wasn't herself. She had always taken pride in her appearance and had such a passion for fashion. Yet lately, she had switched her fancy dresses and blouses for trousers and often a black, long-sleeved polar neck shirt. Her heels were gone, replaced by comfortable ballet pumps. And her hair was scraped back into a high bun. She had also stopped applying makeup, not that she needed it. Benedict thought she looked even more radiant with her natural beauty. Still, he had known Charlotte for most of his life. And from what he remembered from when they were in school, she only wore makeup because she enjoyed the creativity of unique looks. Her smile may have been bright, but her eyes were dull. He knew she was still struggling. He hoped he hadn't pushed her to come back before she was ready.

As the week went on, Charlotte seemed to prefer her own company.

She would collect her coffee from the staff room and hide away in her office. She only opened her door to students and was barely seen wandering the halls between appointments.

"She's probably sick of everyone mollycoddling her. Leave the poor girl alone," Mrs Brown warned the staff.

She had a point. Benedict watched as everyone treated her with kid gloves, and he knew how annoying that could be.

Finally, he knew he had to say something. "Hey, are you free? Can I come in?" he asked, knocking on her door, and popping his head inside.

"Sure, how can I help?" she asked as she fiddled with papers on her desk.

"I just wanted to stop by and see how you are doing. I know you are probably sick of everyone asking, but still...." He smiled, taking a seat in the chair meant for students. It was a little too snug for him to sit comfortably.

"I'm good." She was lying, busying herself again.

"You were always crap at acting," he said.

"Excuse me? As if you saw one of my performances," she said, finally looking his way.

She let out a small chuckle, and he was overjoyed to see her struggling to suppress a grin.

"I see what you did there. Touché, Mr Sterling."

Benedict shrugged and held up his hands in mock surrender. "Me? I know not of what you speak. I am but a simple man in the presence of a beautiful woman. I mean no harm or malice. I simply am," he said, quoting a line from one of the drama productions he had watched so many years ago.

"I can't believe you remembered that," she said, shaking her head.

"I am but a simple man with a simple life. Hoping the beautiful woman would honour me with her presence Friday evening." He grinned.

"I don't think that was the next line," she said, eyeing him with suspicion but clearly enjoying herself.

"Wasn't it?.... Maybe it was just my goofy way of asking you out on a date."

Charlotte's face blanked, and her eyes grew wide. Benedict worried he had crossed a line.

"Are you asking me out?"

"Yes." He answered simply, half holding his breath as he waited for her reply.

Her face softened, and slowly her smile lit up her face.

"I thought you would never ask," she grinned.

"Really?" he asked in complete bemusement.

"What time?"

Chapter Sixteen

FERNBROOK WAS A SMALL TOWN, and after everything that had happened as of late, Benedict wanted their date to be intimate and private. He didn't want to risk running into anyone they knew, especially anyone from work. So, he booked a table at Viva La Mexico by Lake Windemere, an hour and a half drive from Fernbrook. While it would be a long drive, he knew it would be worth it.

After school, he and Charlotte went home to get changed. Benedict told her he would pick her up at six. Benedict didn't date much and found he was overly worried. What should he wear? Should he put on a dab of cologne? What should he talk about? His stomach flipped, and he worried that he'd be so nervous he wouldn't be able to eat. Finally, he settled on a simple pair of dark blue jeans and a black fitted shirt left open at the collar. He tamed his hair and dabbed a few drops of his only fancy cologne before grabbing his grandfather's Rolex and sliding it onto his wrist. Satisfied, he looked in the mirror one last time before dashing out and making the short drive to Charlotte's house.

He stood at her door for a good minute before finally taking a breath and knocking. He didn't wait long before she answered. His jaw dropped at the sight of her. She wore an elegant, figure-hugging cocktail dress with red leather high heels and a matching red bag with a silver shoulder strap. Her makeup was perfect, and her hair fell in loose waves down her back. He could see now why her modelling career had been so successful even if it was short. She was a vision.

"What's wrong?" she asked, searching the blank look on his face.

"Char, you look.... wow.... I mean...breathtaking," he finally said.

"You look pretty tasty yourself, Benny." She winked as she turned to lock her door.

He raised one eyebrow at this. "Benny?"

"What? You can give me a cute nickname, but I can't give you one?" she chuckled.

Benedict looked back at her in confusion.

"Char?" she offered when he still said nothing.

"Oh...yeah, I guess I did," he laughed nervously, rubbing the back of his neck.

"So where are we headed?" she asked, following him to his car.

Benedict rushed around to the passenger side to open the door for her.

"Ever the gentleman," she smiled.

"Viva La Mexico," he answered as he fastened himself in.

"That's an hour and a half away," she said in astonishment.

"Have you been there before?"

"No, but I've heard of it."

"I think it will be worth the drive." Benedict smiled.

"Did you enjoy your food, sir?" asked the waitress as she cleared their plates.

"Wonderful, thank you," Benedict offered.

"Truly amazing. I don't think I could eat another bite," Charlotte replied, making the young woman smile before she headed off.

"I like a woman who isn't afraid to eat more than a salad," Benedict said.

"I ate a lot, didn't I? Food is never something I have struggled with. I love food, and that was *definitely* worth the drive." Charlotte smiled.

Benedict paid the bill, even though Charlotte insisted she pay her half. He waited for her to pop into the ladies' room and paid for everything while she was gone. When she got back, she insisted she buy the drinks at the bar, and after a lot of play fighting in one booth tucked into a cosy corner of the bar, he agreed.

Benedict was driving home, so he stuck to soft drinks but encouraged Charlotte to have a drink if she wanted. The conversation flowed freely, and they found they had more in common than they thought. They shared similar tastes in movies and music, and both loved reading, although Charlotte favoured classic novels over his comic books and crime dramas. They both loved to travel and cook and had a talent for DIY. They laughed and joked and shared their opinions on who was their favourite teachers and students—apparently, each other didn't count. Charlotte said it was cheating.

Benedict laughed loudly. "So it's agreed, we both think Siobhan hasn't changed since school?"

Charlotte laughed with him. "Agreed. She is still the same opinionated gossip she was back then," Charlotte raised a glass in a toast to all opinionated gossips. "Caroline told me about what she said and how you defended me. That was really sweet." She whispered, tucking her hair behind her ear coyly.

"I meant every word."

"I shouldn't have stayed locked up for so long, but it was hard. I thought I had escaped my past. I guess not," she offered.

"What do you mean?" Benedict asked.

Charlotte took a long sip of her cocktail before answering. "As you know, Ava was in the pageant business. She pressured me to follow in her footsteps. She prized beauty and poise over everything else. I could never tell her when I got an A or won the rewards program. It wasn't important to her. It was more important to be the perfect wife to a rich husband and raise a family," she began.

"You won the rewards program? I didn't know," Benedict said, shocked to find this out.

The year of their shared science fair experiment, he had won the rewards program. There were two other winners, one being Simon. The other student had requested to stay private. Benedict never expected it to be Charlotte.

"Yeah, I won. Don't sound so surprised," she said, jabbing him in the side with her finger. "I asked the school if we could keep it quiet, so Ava didn't find out. I knew she would disapprove. I used to enjoy the pageants and modelling every now and again, but it was always her dream, not mine. I just looked at it to bond with my mother. I was always jealous of how close my girlfriends were with their parents.... On the day of the science fair, I tried to convince her to let me go. But we got into a huge argument about how she thought I was ungrateful. In the end, what could I do? I went where she wanted me to go. When I got the gig with Central Faces, she got worse. Much worse. She became a tyrant. Nothing I did was ever good enough. I was never pretty enough. I needed to do better than my last gig. She would trot me out like a prized pig to anyone she deemed eligible. Then they realised I was nothing like my mother had described. I guess I wasn't very good at being demure, quiet, and eager to please. Thankfully, when they saw what I was really like, they would leave. She was never happy," Charlotte said.

Benedict noticed how she was struggling and didn't want to upset her, yet he wanted to know more. He needed to better understand who she really was. He liked what he had learned about her so far.

"Before I stopped modelling, we had another argument. I kicked her out and haven't seen her since I moved out of London. That's why I was so scared to leave the house. The guy introduced himself as a friend of Ava's. He told me she had sent him and promised him a date with a former model. He showed me the messages between him and her. She made me out to be desperate for a man. I told him no, and he flipped out," she sighed. Benedict was glad to see it seemed easier for her to talk about the incident now. Hopefully, that meant she was healing from the ordeal.

"I'm so sorry, I had no idea."

"It's okay. No one did. I hid the nature of my relationship with Ava away from everyone."

Benedict was struck with guilt. All those years, he thought she was a stuck-up, spoiled rich kid with the perfect life. He thought she was self-absorbed, obsessed with her looks, and only interested in chasing fame and fortune. When they worked on the science fair project together, he had seen a different side to her. She'd shown him her intelligence and eagerness to learn. He just hadn't noticed it at the time.

"Not just for that, I completely misjudged you all those years ago. Even recently, when you first came back to Fernbrook, I treated you horribly. Char, I'm so sorry. Can you ever forgive me?" he asked.

"Water under the bridge. Better late than never, right?" she winked, patting his knee.

Chapter Seventeen

~~~

BENEDICT CLEARED his throat as he talked. Sharing his story was difficult for him, but it felt right, especially given Charlotte's own raw honesty.

"I was…. not myself back then. As you saw yourself when we worked together. My father was a complicated man. From as young as I can remember, he strived for perfection. I was never performing well enough. Education was the be-all and end-all of his world. One of my earliest memories was just before my mum left," Benedict began.

Charlotte gave his knee a reassuring squeeze and offered a comforting smile. She knew this was hard to discuss, but she also knew that he needed to. She doubted he had ever spoken about his father with anyone.

"I was four. They were screaming. I was crying in my mother's arms as he scolded me for not reading at a high enough level. She left the following year. Dad always blamed me for her going. He told me I was a disappointment, and that she was embarrassed to call me her son. I spent the rest of my school years pushing myself to be what he wanted me to be, so he wouldn't leave too," Benedict confessed.

Charlotte gasped and shifted a little closer to him. Gently, she wrapped her arms around his neck and pulled him close. She inhaled his cologne and stroked the back of his neck. She wanted to make him see he was good enough. He had always been good enough.

"You know it wasn't your fault, right? You have always been amazing. You were always amazing," she said in his ear.

She felt a need to protect him. This strong, intelligent man still housed his childhood's scared feelings of rejection. He slowly wrapped his arm around her and held her close for a while before pulling away. He stroked her cheek with his thumb and looked deep into her eyes, eyes that were screaming how much she cared.

"I know. Their marriage was a disaster before I came along. I just wanted my father to tell me he cared. I got my wish on the day of the science fair. He encouraged me to take credit because you couldn't make it. He never liked the idea that you could do the math that I couldn't."

"Do you still talk to your father?" she asked, hoping he too had escaped a toxic relationship as she had.

"He passed years ago."

"I didn't know. I'm so sorry."

Benedict continued to tell her about how he used his win from the rewards program. He started a tech business because it was what his father wanted, but he was never happy. He told her how he'd let it fail when he moved back to care for his father, and then fell into teaching when he got back in touch with Simon.

"I never thought about teaching, mostly because of my father. Yet I've never been happier," he said. His face lit up when he talked about his students.

"You are an amazing teacher. The kids adore you, and I can see why," she said. "It's funny. The two of us had strained relationships with our parents and lived our lives to please them, only to end up in a completely different field," she grinned.

She felt free while talking with Benedict and confessed about her declining mental state near the end of her relationship with Ava. She told him how she would sit and wonder about all the things Ava had said and done to mould her into the person she had become.

"At my lowest, I referred myself to a therapist, and it gave me a better understanding of my mind and Ava's. After that, I felt free for the first time in my life and decided I wanted to help others who were struggling to find themselves. So, I headed off to university and became a psychologist."

They continued to talk about their pasts until the waiter announced it was time for last call. When they looked out the window, they realised it was very late in the evening. Time certainly flew when you were having fun. Disappointed the night was ending, they strolled to Benedict's car and prepared for the drive home.

Later, as they stood at Charlotte's door, she fidgeted with her keys, hoping for a goodnight kiss. She was too nervous to attempt the first kiss herself, plus she wanted to know if he felt the same. She thought he did from how the evening had been such a success. But Benedict didn't make his move.

Charlotte felt hollow as she locked her door behind her.

Chapter Eighteen

CHARLOTTE COULDN'T STOP THINKING about her date with Benedict. At the end of the date, they agreed to keep their outing a secret to stop unnecessary gossip, mostly from Siobhan. They wanted to explore what was there before they told anyone, and Charlotte was happy with that.

Back in the swing of things at The Northern Swan, the students noticed how she had a spring in her step and a glow about her. A few had seen the same about Benedict too. One student even asked if the pair were an item, commenting on how cute of a couple they would make. Charlotte denied it, but deep down, she rather liked the idea.

Benedict was a much more complicated person than she thought, but she liked a challenge and looked forward to unravelling the mystery that was Benedict.

As the weeks went by, Charlotte noticed a change in him, subtle at first but pleasant. He was softer and smiled a lot more, and slowly he replaced his oversized, ill-fitting suits with much more fashionable and flattering clothes. Part of her hoped he wasn't changing for her, she liked him the way he was. But she couldn't help admiring how his new clothes showed off his trim physique.

They shared their lunch breaks together in the staff room, and both arrived earlier in the morning to share breakfast. Yet there had been no mention on either part regarding a second date.

Charlotte wanted a second date; she had dreamt about their date several times since, and each time she woke up before the goodnight kiss. The goodnight kiss she never got. Instead, she found she would stare longingly at his lips, wondering how they would feel on hers.

Call her old-fashioned, but Charlotte always believed it was the man's job to ask for the date and make a move for the first kiss. It was an ideal of her mother's that she could not shake yet. Here she was, an independent, confident, capable woman. But like most, she enjoyed being chased. She dropped hints here and there, but Benedict didn't seem to pick up on them. So, while she patiently waited for him to ask her out again, she was happy to enjoy the time they spent together and the texts they exchanged.

"BENEDICT, I have to say you look mighty fine these days," Siobhan said as she entered his classroom.

"Thanks," he replied dryly.

It was never Siobhan whom he wanted to notice him. He sat back in his chair, trying to create space between them as she seductively leaned over his desk. She had purposely undone one too many buttons of her blouse to allow her cleavage to show. Benedict, being a gentleman—and someone who was not interested in her advances—kept his eyes firmly on her face.

"I was wondering if you had plans for this weekend. You like whiskey, right? I have a superb bottle back at my place. So maybe you come round, and we see where the night goes?" she purred as she toyed with the stationary on his desk.

Benedict kept his face stern and stood up to get away from her, walking over to the board to write up notes for his next lesson. He glanced at the clock. It approached that time when Charlotte would turn up so they could share lunch together. He didn't want her to get the wrong idea, and he definitely didn't want Siobhan in his classroom.

The sound of pens landing on the floor startled him; he turned and saw Siobhan had climbed up on his desk. He tried to hide his disgust; her attempts to seduce him had become desperate and embarrassing.

"Do you mind?" he said, annoyed as he picked up the papers from the floor.

As he stood and placed everything back on the desk, he hesitated. He wanted to push her off the desk but didn't want to touch her. She reached out and grabbed his tie, pulling him closer.

"Come on, Benedict, don't make me beg," she said, batting her eyelashes.

Out of the corner of his eye, he saw a shadow leaving his doorway, and he knew Charlotte had seen everything.

Charlotte kept her head down as she walked through the halls. She headed to her office and locked the door. She turned off the light and opened the window to allow enough light in the room. A slight breeze drifted through the room, allowing her time to calm down.

Is this why he hasn't asked me on a second date? He has moved on to Siobhan? Of all people, why her? He is just as much a pig as most men, Charlotte thought as she sat at her desk staring at the blank screen on her computer.

Jealousy was a childish emotion. At least that's what she always told herself. She had never had much interest in relationships and told no one about her past. She liked her privacy, yet something about Benedict had made her feel safe. Was it simply because he had shown up the night of the attack? She kicked herself for letting her walls down and promised herself she wouldn't make the same mistake again.

Suddenly, she found she was no longer hungry. Instead, she dove back into old bad habits. Tucked in a pocket in her handbag was a pack of cigarettes. She wasn't a smoker typically. She only ever had one once in a blue moon when she felt stressed or at her lowest. Pulling one out, she perched on the open windowsill and lit up, staring out over the hills of Fernbrook as she smoked.

Chapter Nineteen

LATER THAT DAY, as Benedict went to his car, he saw Charlotte approaching. He smiled at her, but she didn't smile back. Instead, she dropped her gaze and hurried to her car. Confused, and hoping she wasn't still upset by what he suspected she'd seen with Siobhan, he went over to see what was wrong.

"Hey, I missed you at lunch. Everything alright?" he asked.

She mumbled something, but it was too low for Benedict to make out clearly.

"Sorry?" he asked.

"I'm fine, just not feeling too good," she said, jumping in her car and driving off without uttering another word.

When he arrived home, he sent her a text letting her know if she needed anything, all she had to do was call, and that he hoped she felt better soon. He worried when she didn't reply.

The rest of the week was a lot of the same. She was the same old Charlotte but seemed distant and closed off when Benedict was around. He missed her. He had grown accustomed to their brief moments together and was working up the courage to tell her he liked her. Whatever he had done to offend her, he was sure he had lost his chance.

"What's up, dude? You seem different," Simon said as he sat down next to Benedict at lunch.

"Nothing, I'm fine," he lied.

"You and the Mrs have a fight? You two haven't been as close lately," Simon said.

"Mrs?"

"You know. Charlotte. You seemed pretty close," Simon said with a mouthful of food.

"We are not a thing; we never were. Since when have you paid so much attention to my day-to-day life, anyway?" Benedict asked, annoyed to think he'd been the subject of so much interest.

"Everyone thought you were a thing. You were practically inseparable."

Benedict was glad to hear he wasn't imagining things. Everyone else had noticed a change in Charlotte's behaviour lately.

"I heard you turned down Siobhan," Simon said, still chewing his food like a child.

"Let me guess, she told you?" Benedict said, exasperated. He hated gossip, even more when people talked about him. He was a private person, and he liked it that way.

"Are you kidding? The woman practically throws herself at you, and you say no? Yeah, she told anyone who would listen. But, hey, maybe that's why Charlotte isn't talking to you. She doesn't think you're serious," Simon offered.

Simon's words hit Benedict hard. Perhaps he was right. He thought he had seen her in the doorway, but she had left so quickly that she wouldn't have seen him rejecting Siobhan's advances. It had been pretty brutal. Siobhan had even tossed a stapler at him when he'd told her to leave.

The bell rang, and Simon walked with Benedict back to their class-rooms. Simon was still waffling on, but Benedict had tuned him out, nodding along but not really listening until Simon stopped when they spotted Charlotte coming out of her office.

"If you're not hitting that, can I?" Simon said, eyeing Charlotte like she was a piece of meat and he a hungry bear.

"What?" Benedict said, unsure if he had heard his friend correctly.

"She was a model, right? Bet she picked up a few tricks along the way. It would be nice to add an ex-model to my CV," Simon said, rather pleased with himself at his crude and degrading remark.

Benedict looked at Charlotte. She hadn't noticed them. His blood boiled at the thought of anyone thinking those horrid things about her. To hear it from someone he considered a friend was too much. He turned and shoved Simon hard in the shoulder. "Not cool. She's a woman, not an object. Treat her with the respect she deserves. I will not have you talking about her like that," Benedict said, trying to keep his voice low, so the passing students didn't know what was happening.

"Benedict, man. What happened to bros before hoes?" Simon laughed.

That was enough. Unable to control his temper any longer, Benedict swung and landed a punch square in Simon's nose. A loud crack sounded, followed by Simon's muffled cries of pain as he cupped his nose, blood pouring between his fingers. Students gasped and ran away.

"Benedict!" Charlotte shouted as she helped Simon to his feet. "What is wrong with you?"

The look in her eyes pained him. She was angry and disgusted. If he didn't know any better, he would think she hated him. *If only she knew.*

The students had alerted the headmistress to the commotion, and Mrs Brown, her face red with anger, barrelled down the hall. She yelled for Simon and Benedict to get to her office immediately. Like two naughty schoolboys, they followed her to her office where they had to listen to her lecture them about appropriate behaviour for the next hour.

Leaving Mrs Brown's office, Benedict found Charlotte waiting, her hands folded across her chest and a look of thunder on her face.

"My office. Now!" she spat, storming off, not waiting to see if he followed.

She was pacing her office like a caged animal when he arrived. He sat in the all too small chair in front of her desk and ran his hands through his hair. He had already received a tongue lashing and a three-week suspension without pay from Mrs Brown. He didn't have the energy to take much more.

"What the heck was that all about? I've had terrified students banging on my door. No doubt I will have a string of angry parents wanting to talk with me now, and of course, I will have to do a psychological evaluation to make sure it's safe for you to continue working with kids after this," she rambled, still furious.

"He had it coming. I wasn't going to stand there and let him say those things about you," he mumbled.

He hadn't meant for Charlotte to hear that last part. But by the way she paused and sat down, he knew she had. He buried his face in his hands and sighed, leaning his arms on his knees. It had been a long day.

"What did you just say?" she breathed, her voice barely a whisper.

Reluctantly, he relayed what Simon had said and felt his temper flaring again. It wasn't until he looked into her eyes that he calmed down.

"Why did you do that? Why do you care? I'm a grown woman. I can handle myself," she said, clearly frustrated.

"Because I like you, Charlotte. I mean, *really* like you. I've never felt like this before, and it's scaring me. I wasn't going to stand by and let him say such disgusting things. I told him to stop, but he wouldn't. He needed to know he can't talk about you, or anyone really, like that," he said as he paced the small room.

Charlotte said nothing. He was aware of her watching him as he paced.

"I've spent all week trying to figure out what I did to offend or upset you. We seemed to get along great. I thought you felt the same way, but then you pushed me away," he said finally, figuring he may as well get it all out there since she was already mad.

"What about Siobhan? I saw you two in your classroom...."

Benedict interrupted her. "I knew you had. I thought I saw you at the door. If you had stuck around, you would have seen me tell her I had no interest in her. That I thought her display was distasteful, and I wasn't interested in anyone but.... you."

"I wondered why she kept shooting me dirty looks all week," Charlotte smirked. "If you like me, why didn't you say anything? We are adults after all."

"Why didn't you say anything to me?" he asked right back. Turnabout was fair play.

"Touché." She grinned.

They arranged their second date then and there, each feeling the same rush of excitement as before.

Chapter Twenty

CHARLOTTE WANTED to wait until the heat had died down from the Simon incident until they went on their date. Also, Mrs Brown told all the teachers to have no contact with Benedict until after his suspension. However, that didn't stop either Benedict or Charlotte from texting and calling every day. Charlotte found she looked forward to her good morning texts and good night messages from Benedict. Even though she knew she shouldn't, she also kept him updated on his students.

After his suspension ended, they were more than happy to be seen together in Fernbrook, no longer feeling the need to hide away since they had both admitted they liked each other.

Benedict wanted to show Charlotte something special, so he took her out on the lake in his father's old boat. She could sail herself but was happy to let him take the lead.

After enjoying a beautiful sunny day on the calming waters of West Lake, they settled in for dinner at The Lake House. A few of the other teachers and town gossips kept spying on them, and they had fun acting up just to give them something to gossip about. Playfully, they fed each other dessert. Benedict hooked himself around Charlotte while they played pool. They even crashed a private party in the function room, recreating their karaoke moment from the end-of-year party. At that point, the guests had realised they were not invited, and they were asked to leave.

They laughed uncontrollably as they fell out of The Lake House.

"That was so much fun. I can't believe we crashed that party," Charlotte howled, holding her sides which hurt from laughing.

Benedict laughed with her. "Crashed? We made that party what it was. Did you hear them singing before we jumped on stage? We killed it!"

Benedict stopped to watch as Charlotte laughed. Her eyes creased, and her smile was brighter than he had ever seen. She looked stunning under a mix of the moon's glow and the coloured string of lights that trailed around the door frame. Stepping closer, he pulled her close and hooked his hand around the back of her neck. Even in her high heels, Benedict towered over her. She knew what was coming. She pulled him closer as he brought his lips down on hers. It was a gentle yet passionate kiss, full of promise and unspoken words. It was a kiss Charlotte would remember forever, and one she didn't want to end.

As Benedict walked her home, being the gentleman, he offered her his jacket when it grew cold. Charlotte couldn't remember a time she had had so much fun. Her cheeks hurt from smiling and laughing all night, and she savoured his scent as she hooked her arm in his on the scenic walk home. If she didn't know any better, she would say she was living in a fairy tale.

But in every good fairy tale, there is always a villain waiting to steal the princess' happiness. This night was no exception. Benedict and Charlotte rounded the corner of cosy cottages with lush, full lawns, nearing where Charlotte lived. A car parked at the end of her driveway caused her to halt in her steps.

"What's wrong?" Benedict asked as her grip on his arm tightened.

"How did she find me?" she breathed as a tall, slender woman with golden hair walked back up the path from Charlotte's front door towards the car.

"Is that?...."

"Ava," Charlotte finished as her mother spotted them and waved excitedly in their direction.

Chapter Twenty-One

CHARLOTTE WATCHED as Ava slowly walked up the street towards her and Benedict. Her heart pounded in her chest. She felt Benedict's grip on her tighten as her hands shook. She had such a lovely evening with Benedict, and now it was ruined.

"Charlotte Darling. I'm so happy to see you," Ava chimed as she drew closer.

Charlotte's blood boiled. How could Ava act as though all those years hadn't happened? How could she be so brazen?

"How did you find me?" Charlotte asked.

"What? Not even a helo, mum? Nice to see you, mum?" Ava asked with a smile, opening her arms wide for a hug.

Charlotte never let go of Benedict's hand, as she stepped back out of her mother's reach.

"Go away, Ava," Charlotte said dryly.

She pulled gently on Benedict's hand, pulling him towards her home. She wanted to get inside and lock Ava out. She didn't have the energy or patience to deal with Ava anymore.

"Please, Charlotte, just listen to me," Ava called after them.

"Go away, Ava," Charlotte yelled back.

Benedict and Charlotte went inside, and Charlotte quickly locked the door. However, it wasn't long before Ava started making a scene. She hammered her fist on the door and yelled through the letterbox.

"Your neighbours will start watching if she carries on like that," Benedict said as he pulled the curtain back to peer out and see what Ava was doing.

Charlotte pushed him aside and closed the curtains. She knew he was right, but still, that didn't mean she wanted Ava in her home. Reluctantly, she opened the door. Benedict had been right. Charlotte saw several of her neighbours peeking through their curtains. *Great, I will be the gossip of Fernbrook by morning,* she thought. With no other choice, she grabbed Ava by the arm and dragged her inside.

"Say what you have to say and then leave," Charlotte said.

Ava attempted to move past Charlotte and enter the living room, but Charlotte kept stepping in her way. The hallway was the only part of the house she would allow Ava to enter.

"Look, darling, I know we ended things badly. I will even admit to my part in our petty squabble. I just want my daughter back," Ava pleaded.

"You gave up that right the second you promised me to that creep who attacked me. How did you find me? How did you know I'd move back here? My address is unlisted." Charlotte asked, folding her arms across her chest, and staring Ava down.

"I did no such thing," Ava gasped. Even Benedict could surmise how fake her response was.

"Answer the question!" Charlotte snapped.

Ava stared back at her daughter's outburst. "Fine, I hired a private investigator. It wasn't hard, though, after you appeared in the newspaper," Ava answered.

"So, you thought you would get back in touch by offering me out to some pervert. What part of that did you think would make me want anything to do with you? Did you think I would be happy? Did you think I would beg for him to tell me where you were?" Charlotte asked her blood boiling.

She had forgotten Benedict was there. She would have controlled her temper better if she remembered.

"I didn't send him," Ava said pointing over Charlotte's shoulder towards Benedict. "I don't even know who he is."

"I'm talking about the creep who came looking for me last month," Charlotte snapped.

"Oh, him. Well, I never intended for him to go looking. He was actually the private investigator's son. I will have words with him, don't you worry about that. Anyway, darling, as I said, I'm so sorry for my behaviour. These past few years have been so empty without you. I want to have a relationship with you again. I miss my little Lottie," Ava said, but her words rang hollow.

Charlotte knew her mother well enough to know when she was being fake and insincere. And she always hated the nickname, Lottie.

"Don't call me that! I'm through with you, Ava. Now get out of my house, and if I see you around here again, I'm calling the police," Charlotte snarled through gritted teeth as she opened the door and pushed her mum back out onto the porch, slamming the door behind her.

She listened as Ava's footsteps grew fainter and sighed a breath of relief when she heard a car engine start and drive away. She sank into the door, suddenly feeling a lot heavier and desperate for a drink and a smoke.

Benedict crept out of the doorway and walked over. Saying nothing, he took Charlotte into his arms and held her close. She felt so safe with Benedict that she let the tears fall as she sobbed. She cried about the lost relationship, her anger, and her frustration. Deep down, she knew history was about to repeat itself.

Benedict led Charlotte through to the kitchen. He scooped her up and sat her on the counter while he busied himself making tea.

"Are you going to be OK?" he asked as he bustled about the kitchen.

"Not really, no. I'm sorry, I don't normally do this, especially on a second date, but you are about to see my worst feature," she answered.

Confused, Benedict watched as she pulled open the drawer and pulled out a pack of cigarettes.

"I didn't know you smoked," he said, more alarmed than he intended.

"I don't usually. I have one once in a blue moon. When I'm overly stressed." She paused. "Ava brings out the worst in me," she said, lighting up and heading for the back door.

She opened the door and stood halfway between the kitchen and the back garden, allowing the smoke to billow outside. Benedict said nothing as he continued to make the tea.

"I'm sorry you had to see that," Charlotte eventually said, trying to break the silence.

"I'm just glad I was here. After explaining what she put you through, I couldn't imagine you coming home alone and finding her here. Do you think she was serious about wanting a relationship with you again?" he asked, placing her tea on the counter closest to her.

She smiled her thanks and took another drag, thinking over his question before answering.

"No. I think she has run out of money and milked her connections dry. I think she misses the old life and wants to use me to get it back. Like I'm some prized poodle," Charlotte answered.

Benedict kept his expression under control, but it pained him at how little emotion there was in Charlotte's voice as she answered. Was it how cold she was towards Ava that bothered him? Or that he knew her answer was right.

"Would you want a relationship with her again?"

"No, I've been through that once. Never again," she lied.

While she didn't want to go through all the toxic drama of last time, a small part of her still wanted Ava to be part of her life. Deep down, she was still little Lottie wishing to please her mother. Little Lottie, jealous of the relationships her friends had with their mothers.

"I know we have only been on two dates, but I'm here for you, and I will support you whatever you choose," Benedict said.

Charlotte tossed the end of her smoke out the door and took a sip of her tea. She smiled at him when she saw his sincerity and wrapped her arms around him.

"Thank you, I really appreciate it."

Chapter Twenty-Two

Ava was a stubborn old mule and continued to turn up at Charlotte's house. She would be there when she arrived home from work and occasionally would show up first thing in the morning before she left. Charlotte felt her stress levels building as she kept insisting Ava leave her alone. Still, the more Ava turned up, the more Charlotte felt obligated to at least hear her out.

After two weeks, Ava stopped coming around, and Charlotte worried. Where had she gone? Was Ava OK? She missed seeing Ava, even if she didn't always want to talk to her. She had quickly gotten used to Ava being back in her life.

Another week passed with no sign of Ava. Charlotte couldn't help herself and searched for her on social media as she didn't have a contact number. It didn't take long to find Ava's Facebook, but it looked like she hadn't used it in years. Nevertheless, Charlotte hoped Ava still logged in occasionally and sent her a message. Whenever Charlotte's phone pinged for the rest of the day, her heart leapt in her chest, hoping it was Ava. When it wasn't, she felt deflated.

"Hey there, you OK?" Benedict asked, entering her office.

She smiled to see him. "Hey you, yeah, I'm fine. How is your day going?"

Benedict looked at her for a moment before sitting down. He sat back in the all too small chair, despite Ava bringing in a bigger chair for him since he had spent so much time in her office of late.

"Don't say it, Benny," she said, turning back to her phone.

"I wasn't going to say anything." He grinned.

"Yes, you were. You were about to say, I'm not fine. Sometimes I hate how easy it is for you to read me," she complained.

Secretly she loved it. Benedict had been her rock since Ava's return. She appreciated he sat and listened to her seemingly endless venting and the way he provided constant words of support.

"I didn't need to say anything. You just admitted you are not okay."

"I hate you," she teased, as she grinned back at him. "It's Ava. I haven't heard from her, and I'm worrying. She is never one to give up easy."

"Didn't you tell her to go away?" he asked, clearly confused.

"Yes, but normally she would protest harder and at least say good-bye," Charlotte complained.

"She's manipulating you. She is trying to make you worry, so you're the one to make contact...." Benedict stopped when he saw the look on Charlotte's face. She never could hide something from him. Not since they had officially become an item, anyway. "You made contact, didn't you?" he asked.

"Benedict, please."

"I'm not saying anything. I said I would support you, and that's what I will do. But you can't deny the fact that I'm right."

"I know." She sighed.

Benedict convinced Charlotte to stop staring at her screen, waiting for a reply that may or may not come. Charlotte wasn't in the mood to be dealing with the likes of Siobhan or Simon—things were still awkward between them all—so Benedict suggested they head to a local cafe for lunch. Charlotte welcomed the change of scenery as they headed to the car park together.

Their students had quickly realised that they were now a couple and had taken to wolf-whistling as they walked by with some boys offering a chorus of, "Get in there, sir! She is a beauty."

It was a beautiful sunny day, but as always, there was a chill in the breeze in the UK. Still, that didn't stop Benedict and Charlotte from enjoying lunch outside, watching all the boats sail on West Water Lake. It was just the distraction Charlotte needed. She knew Benedict was right about Ava, but that didn't stop the nagging voice in the back of her head.

"We better head back. Classes will start again soon," Benedict said as he paid the bill.

"I'm just going to pop to the ladies. I'll be right back." Charlotte excused herself and went inside.

As she passed the cakes counter, she thought she saw a familiar face in the crowd but brushed the thought away. It wasn't until she was fixing her makeup in the bathroom mirror she realised who she had seen. Just then, Ava walked in. They locked eyes in the mirror, momentarily frozen.

"Hello," Ava said, slowly breaking out into a sweet, tentative smile.

"Where the heck have you been? I've been worried sick," Charlotte snapped, spinning around so fast she almost lost her footing.

"You told me to leave you alone. I thought I was doing what you wanted," Ava replied.

"Don't do that. You know exactly what you are doing. No goodbye, nothing. I had no way to contact you."

"I didn't know you cared so much," Ava interrupted the corners of her mouth twitching as she struggled to suppress a grin.

"Despite our differences, you are still my mother," Charlotte huffed, rolling her eyes.

"Look, I know I haven't been the best mum. But I really would like to try to be better, to do better. All I ask is you give me a chance. Here is my card. I won't bother you any further. If you want to talk, just call." Ava left without another word, almost as if she had followed Charlotte inside on purpose.

Charlotte looked at the card, suddenly unsure of how she felt. Her mother's name and phone number were followed by a job title she should have expected. *Still, in the pageant business, I see. Some things never change.*

Charlotte and Ava agreed to take things slowly as the weeks went by. Occasionally, they would meet for coffee or lunch and even went out to dinner once or twice. Whenever it seemed they were making progress and Charlotte believed Ava had changed, Ava would ghost Charlotte for a few days, not answering Charlotte's calls or texts and suddenly appearing again as if nothing had happened.

Benedict could see the games Ava was playing, but no matter how much he warned Charlotte, she wouldn't listen. Benedict worried Charlotte would get hurt, but he also loved seeing how happy she was that she finally had a relationship with her mother. He knew this was something she had craved for years. He understood the need to connect. It was a biological need, something out of Charlotte's control. Deep down, everyone wanted to be loved unconditionally, especially by a parent. Of course, Charlotte would want that too.

"Please, just be careful. I don't like the way she is manipulating you. She gives you enough, then vanishes, and how do you react? You go running back. You're even helping her with her business again. How long before she tries to get you to...I don't know, leave the school? I just don't want you getting hurt," Benedict said one night after yet another beautiful date night.

"You're paranoid. She's just being Ava. That's who she is. I know how to handle her. Plus, she's busy with work herself. It's pageant season, after all. But I appreciate how much you care," Charlotte replied, kissing him softly goodnight.

Chapter Twenty-Three

For Charlotte's sake alone, Benedict tried to be civil with Ava. He would greet her politely when he was around and play nice as best he could. Charlotte was fooled, believing the two were getting along, but Ava's demeanour towards Benedict changed whenever Charlotte wasn't around. She did not try to hide the snide looks she shot in his direction or how she looked down her nose at him.

Benedict didn't want to upset Charlotte, so he bit his tongue and kept his true opinion of Ava to himself. He could see right through her charade and hoped Charlotte would too. Soon. Before it was too late.

"I'll leave you two lovely ladies to it. I have a few things I need to sort at home. I'll see you tomorrow," Benedict said, kissing Charlotte softly.

"It was lovely to see you again, Benny," Ava said.

Charlotte missed it, but Benedict heard the patronising tone she always put into Charlotte's cute nickname for him. The disdain was palpable. How Charlotte had not noticed was beyond him.

"Likewise, Ava," he replied with a smile before leaving mother and daughter to enjoy the rest of their weekend.

"So, Benedict. Not the type of guy I would have imagined you with," Ava said, fiddling with an imaginary piece of thread on her skirt.

"How do you mean?" Charlotte asked.

"You know. Some guys you have dated in the past had much more going for them than just working in a school. He isn't even the head teacher. He is the deputy head. Second in command, so to speak."

"Mum, I work at the same school," Charlotte shot back.

"Yes, but you, my darling, are a psychologist. You could up and leave and travel anywhere with your skills. He will only ever be a teacher."

"He has more going for him than that, mum. He is one of the most intelligent men I have ever met," Charlotte said, defending her choice in Benedict.

"Ah! Yes, the boy-genius, how could I forget?"

"Enough, mother. I like him. That's all that matters," Charlotte said, hoping the discussion was finished.

"I just don't want you to end up like me," Ava said, her voice sadder than Charlotte had heard in a long time.

"What do you mean?"

"I never told you about your father, did I?" Ava asked.

Charlotte simply replied with a sombre shake of the head. She had always wondered but never asked.

"I won't bore you with the details. Plus, I don't want to tarnish the memories you have of your father. But let's just say he was a lot like Benedict. I had a beautiful connection with him I have failed to find with anyone else, and I have been alone ever since," Ava said, putting on her best damsel in destress performance.

Charlotte chuckled. "Thanks for the concern, but I think Benedict and I will be fine. Plus, it's only been a couple of months. It's not like we are getting married, so relax."

CHARLOTTE CONTINUED to help Ava with her pageant business, where she had set up shop in their hometown. However, with her newfound experience working with the students from The Northern Swan, she quickly realised that she could help the young girls a lot more than she initially thought. Having been a student of Ava's herself, Charlotte knew how much hard work there could be in preparing for a beauty pageant. Ava quickly noticed how much the girls flourished under Charlotte's guidance. And Charlotte realised she loved seeing the girls conquer their fears and blossom.

"Darling, you are so wonderful with these girls. I have never seen them happier, and they are performing leaps and bounds ahead of what I expected. Thank you so much for your help," Ava cheered, bringing Charlotte into an enveloping hug.

"Glad I can help," Charlotte smiled. She clung to Ava, inhaling her floral Channel perfume.

"Charlotte, can you help me with my walk? I keep tripping over my dress," Lilly complained.

"Sure thing, sweetie," Charlotte answered.

She strode over with confidence, and the entire room stopped to watch. She wrapped a spare piece of fabric around her waist to show Lilly the best way to hold the skirt to prevent her from tripping and did her best runway strut down the makeshift catwalk in the middle of Ava's workspace. She encouraged Lilly to try, and after a few adjustments, the young girl mastered the walk. She cheered and wrapped her arms around Charlotte's waist, beaming with gratitude and happiness. Charlotte's heart grew with warmth. She loved working with these girls more than she had ever expected to.

"Darling, you are a natural. Why don't you go back into modelling? You're wasting your talents at that school. You could still use your qualifications to help teach other girls, so no worries about wasted school years," Ava chimed as a crowd of mothers arrived to collect their daughters.

"I enjoy working at The Northern Swan. Besides, I've been out of the modelling scene for so long, I don't even have any connections anymore," Charlotte answered.

"I do," Ava grinned.

That wasn't Ava's first, or last, attempt to get Charlotte back on the runway. To Charlotte's surprise, she didn't mind it so much this time. Ava appeared to accept her wishes about not leaving the school, but that didn't stop her from arranging the odd part-time modelling gig here and there. As Charlotte spent a lot more of her spare time helping Ava and travelling to neighbouring cities for gigs, she found the only time she spent with Benedict was at school. Guilt plagued her. She didn't mean to push him aside and didn't want to lose him. He never once complained, constantly offering words of support, and sending flowers every weekend.

"I promise I will make time for us. Do you have anything planned for Saturday?" Charlotte asked.

"Yeah, I have plans with Joe from the gym. I'm taking him out on the lake. The guy has lived in Fernbrook for almost a decade and has never been out on the lake. Can you believe it?"

"Seriously? It's like a rite of passage if you're living in Fernbrook." Charlotte laughed. "You could stay over Friday. We could go out for breakfast before your day of boating with the boys."

"That sounds good," Benedict smirked, wrapping himself around her and burying his face in the crook of her neck, tickling her sides as he did to make her laugh in that way that made him melt.

Chapter Twenty-Four

BENEDICT COULDN'T HELP but notice how Charlotte had been missing a day here and there from school. Worse, she didn't seem present when she was there. It appeared her mind was always on other things. She'd begun focusing on little details, like how she dressed and the way she walked. After a time, he felt he was looking at the Charlotte he had known fifteen years prior.

Shrugging off his concerns, he left school and headed straight for her house. He was happy to see Ava's car wasn't there when he arrived.

"Hey you, what a pleasant surprise. Come in." Charlotte smiled, kissing Benedict gently on the cheek and moving aside for him to enter.

"I'm a little worried, Char. You have missed a lot of school hours lately. Mrs. Brown is letting it slide for now, but I don't know how much longer you can skip and expect to keep your job," Benedict said.

He tried to speak his concerns as softly as he could. He never wanted Charlotte to think of him as being controlling. He was genuinely concerned for her job.

"I know. I'm so sorry. I will call Mrs. Brown tomorrow. Things will be back to normal asap," she answered, but Benedict could tell she wasn't really paying attention.

"So, I take it you won't be at work tomorrow either?" he asked.

"No.... I have a gig," she answered as she fixed her hair in the mirror.

Benedict rolled his eyes and once again bit his tongue. A knock on the door had his mind racing. Things were about to get a lot worse. He wasn't sure how much more of Ava's influence he could take. He had tried not to let Ava impede his feelings for Charlotte, but she was making it increasingly difficult.

"Darling, all set for.... Oh, Benny, how nice to see you," Ava said when her eyes locked on Benedict leaning against the door frame.

"Ditto, Ava," he replied dryly.

At Charlotte's sharp look, it was clear his less than welcoming attitude had not gone unnoticed. The last thing he wanted was to get her back up. *Time to leave.*

"I'll get out of your hair. I hope to see you back at work soon," Benedict smiled, placing a kiss on Charlotte's forehead.

Ava's face darkened. She stepped in front of Benedict and stopped him from leaving.

"Excuse me! Do not tell my daughter what to do," Ava snapped.

"I wasn't," he replied dryly, trying to move past her in the small hallway.

But Ava wasn't letting him leave without a fight. "I told you, Lottie, he is just like your father. Trying to stop you from going for your dreams. He wants to control you," Ava yelled.

"Ava, I am not trying to control Charlotte at all. Even if I was, you raised her well enough that she can take care of herself. She would put me in my place if I tried anything funny."

"He's right, mum," Charlotte winked with a cheeky grin, showing Benedict a flash of the Charlotte he loved.

"Darling, you are so blinded by love you don't see it. He wants to hold you back, to restrict your life to this small town, just like he is," Ava said.

"The only thing she is blinded by is *you*," Benedict finally snapped.

"Excuse me?" Ava asked, feigning ignorance.

"She was doing just fine until you came along and started playing mind games. You hurt her once. I won't let you do it again. I have done nothing but support your daughter, and that's what I intend to continue doing," Benedict said, trying his best not to yell at Charlotte's mother.

"Benedict, please," Charlotte pleaded, looking from him to her mother and back again with distress.

Benedict looked back at Ava and knew he had given her exactly what she wanted. Her face changed, and her eyes flashed with malicious intent.

"Do you see this, Charlotte? Better for you to see his true colours now than years down the line. You have a temper, don't you, Benny?"

"Don't call me that!" Benedict said through gritted teeth.

"Talking to your girlfriend's mother in such a way. So terrible. No respect at all," Ava said, pushing past him to join her daughter.

"OK, I will play your game. You are right. I do not respect you. I tolerate you because I know how much Char cares for you. But I see right through you, Ava. You will use her for your own selfish game and then bounce once you have enough. Or will you stick around and continue to leech off her this time?" Benedict snapped.

"I have my own business, dear. You are merely a teacher. If anything, you are the one leeching off my daughter and her lifestyle."

The fighting escalated quickly. Nasty remarks on both sides flew through the air, and neither Benedict nor Ava cared to listen to Charlotte's protests. Benedict's argument was solely based on exposing Ava for the leech she was. Still, Ava was a master manipulator and always flipped his comments around to make it seem like he was attacking her and her daughter.

"Enough!" Charlotte finally cried, her eyes brimming with tears, "The pair of you are acting like I am not even here. Benedict, I thought I knew you, but mum is right. I should have seen your true colours earlier. Punching Simon was one thing, but attacking my mum like this? I think you should go," Charlotte croaked, her voice cracking as she ushered him out the door.

"What? Char, I was...I never meant...." Benedict fumbled to find the words to fix this.

His chest tightened at the thought of losing her. His hands trembled, and his mind raced as his temper boiled under the surface. He glanced over her shoulder as Ava smirked back at him, waving and mouthing, 'Goodbye, Benny.'

"I will call you soon, but please don't call me. I need time to process everything that happened today," Charlotte whispered, trying her best not to cry.

Benedict reached up to wipe away a stray tear; his heart broke when she tensed at his touch. He never wanted to make her feel like this. In hindsight, he could have handled the situation with Ava a lot better. Still, the woman had a talent for getting under people's skin.

"OK, if that's what you want," he said, but his legs wouldn't let him leave. So he stood memorising the pain in her eyes and the tears he had made fall. He never wanted to see that look again, if she ever returned to him.

"Please, go." She breathed the words and turned, looking back as she closed the door behind her.

Charlotte kept her promise and called Mrs. Brown the following day. She dropped to working part-time, so she could help Ava and attend modelling gigs. The students were disappointed but glad that she was still there, even if it was only three days a week. Benedict kept his distance and waited for her to reach out. But as time passed, he felt a void between them grow. She said hello in the staff room and interacted with him as she did with her other colleagues, but that was it. He had lost her.

Chapter Twenty-Five

AVA HAD TRIED everything she could to convince Charlotte to give up on The Northern Swan. As long as she was tied to the school, she had a connection to Benedict. And Ava knew it wouldn't be long before Charlotte went back to him. She noticed how her daughter longed for him and how much she missed him. Their connection was undeniable. And while he was a good choice for Charlotte, he was a detriment to Ava's plans.

The day finally came when Ava strode through the halls of The Northern Swan, staring down her nose at the halls full of students. She stopped in front of the trophy cabinet and stared at the newspaper article framed next to the school's latest science fair trophy. Benedict and Charlotte smiled next to each other. Ava knew the only way to get Charlotte to do what she wanted was to get her alone. Away from Benedict.

"Mum? What are you doing here?" Charlotte chirped as she walked down the hall towards her.

"I came to see what all the fuss is about. You seem so attached to this place. I wanted to see what made you so happy," Ava beamed, pointing at the trophy cabinet. "You finally made it to the science fair. I didn't know you were so involved in the school's first win back then."

"Yeah, I couldn't make it. It was the same day as my audition for

Central Faces," Charlotte answered, linking her arm in her mother's and walking her towards the staff room.

"Even back then, you were too good for him. I read how he finally gave you credit for the maths he couldn't do. Who would have thought the boy-genius had been bested by my daughter?"

"Mum, stop it. I like Benedict, and I won't stand by and listen to your jibes anymore," Charlotte insisted.

"You can't like him that much. You have hardly spoken to him lately."

"Look, my relationship is my business, not yours. Now come on, let me introduce you to my colleagues and then I will show you around the school and introduce you to some of my students," Charlotte said, walking with a spring in her step.

Ava could see how happy Charlotte was, and it was hard not to notice all the words of admiration the students shot her way as she walked past. She was doing a great job at the school and the love the students had for her. Ava wasn't surprised one bit. She had seen the wonders Charlotte had worked with the pageant girls. Still, she wondered what difference her daughter had made to the lives of these other kids, whom she worked with day after day.

Charlotte introduced Ava to everyone in the staff room and then took her to the head teacher's office to introduce her to Mrs. Brown. Charlotte beamed with happiness; a happiness Ava hadn't seen before. A small part of her in the back of her mind almost made Ava rethink her plans. But the moment she saw Benedict walking down the hall towards them, the voice in her head fell silent.

"Mum, can you find your way back to the staff room? I need to talk to Benedict," Charlotte asked.

"Of course, dear," Ava said, turning her nose up at Benedict as she walked past him.

Ava couldn't cause a scene at the school. Charlotte wouldn't forgive her for that. Instead, she needed a new plan to make Charlotte align with her again, something drastic to get rid of Benedict. She walked into the staff room and took a seat by the window, patiently waiting for Charlotte to finish her chat when a tall, rather attractive woman walked towards her.

"I don't think we have been properly introduced. I'm Siobhan, the drama teacher. Simon tells me you're Charlotte's mother." Siobhan smiled, holding out her hand for Ava to shake.

This is perfect; I've heard a lot about this Siobhan woman. She might be exactly what I need, Ava thought, standing up to shake her new friend's hand.

Chapter Twenty-Six

BENEDICT AND CHARLOTTE walked back to the staff room just as Ava was leaving. Benedict didn't have the patience to be dealing with Ava but smiled at her for Charlotte's sake. After their talk, he was relieved to find that he hadn't lost Charlotte after all. And he didn't want to do anything that could jeopardise their relationship. So, he made a decision to try to be nicer to Ava.

"Just the man I was hoping to see," Ava chirped at their arrival.

"Really?" Charlotte asked, just as surprised as Benedict.

"Yes. Look, I want to apologise. While some things you said to me were out of line, I will admit I was just as much to blame as you. You must understand that while I might not have been the best mother in the past, Charlotte is my primary concern. I just want the best for her, as any parent would. Seeing the work she is doing for these kids and how happy she clearly is, not just here, but with you.... makes things clearer," Ava began.

Benedict stood listening but not genuinely believing or trusting the words leaving her mouth. Then he caught a look at Charlotte out of the corner of his eye and saw the smile growing on her face.

Step carefully here. One wrong word and this whole thing blows up again. Benedict breathed.

He smiled. "I couldn't agree more. Charlotte is a wonderful woman, and I hope you can understand that I want the best for her. I only say what I do because I love her and want to keep her safe. If anyone tried to hurt her, even you, I would want to protect her. But I should have handled things a lot better.... I guess this is what happens when two people love the same person so much."

He froze. His eyes grew wide as he, Charlotte, and Ava realised what he had just said. He hadn't even said those words aloud to himself, let alone to Charlotte. It was too late to take the incriminating word back now. He could only hope she felt the same.

"You.... *love* me?" Charlotte breathed, her expression rapt.

"Of course I do. It might not have been the way I wanted to tell you, but I do. I love you, Charlotte," he said, pouring everything he had into the last words.

Charlotte's face lit up with joy, her eyes sparkling back at him. She took his hand in hers and squeezed gently. "I love you too."

It was everything he had wanted to hear and more. He realised that all the years of seeking approval from others meant nothing compared to the love he now felt. Finally, he had found his person. She was the one person to accept him for the simple man he was, warts and all.

"Well. I guess we better be getting along with each other, hadn't we, Benny?" Ava smiled, and for the first time, she said his nickname without the venom he had become used to hearing.

"I believe we shall. How about we all go out to dinner one night this week? Start anew?" Benedict asked, his eyes not leaving Charlotte's.

He was aware they were surrounded by students rushing to lessons and that Ava was watching. Still, with Charlotte's eyes lovingly staring back at him, he felt like they were the only two people in the world. She was his world now.

It was a little awkward having dinner in the local Italian restaurant with Charlotte and her mother. It was such an odd combination. But Ava was attempting to get along with Benedict. He found the more of her softer side he saw, the more he could see why Charlotte wanted her back in her life. So now that the 'I love yous' were out of the way, Benedict wanted nothing more than to do everything to make Charlotte as happy as she made him. If that meant getting along with Ava, well, so be it.

CHARLOTTE WAS ON CLOUD NINE. Every time she was alone and had nothing to do, her mind drifted back to the moment Benedict had said the three words every woman longs to hear—'I love you.' It meant so much more to her he had said it in front of everyone. To Charlotte, that meant he meant it. He wasn't saying it in private to hide it away and deny it later. He meant every syllable.

Every time she relived that memory, she would feel a blush warm her cheeks and a Cheshire cat-sized grin taking over her face. She was like a love-struck schoolgirl. They had discussed how much Benedict didn't exactly like Ava. Even though she would have liked it if he didn't feel that way, she appreciated his honesty. It meant even more to her that the two most important people in her life had put their differences aside for her.

What more could she want? She sat back and sighed; she had everything she ever wanted. She had a relationship with her mother, a man who loved her, and not only one job she loved, but two. *I'm the luckiest woman alive*, she thought.

She didn't have another student to counsel until after lunch and had caught up on all her paperwork. She knew Benedict had a free period and took advantage of the empty halls before the lunch bell rang. The halls were always silent like this while all the classes were in session. The only sound in the deserted halls was her soft humming and her heels clicking on the marble floors. When she reached Benedict's office, the door was open. Reaching for it she stopped when she heard two voices inside. She knew it was rude to eavesdrop, but she couldn't help herself.

"Oh Benedict, we can't. What if someone sees?" purred Siobhan's voice.

"There is nothing to see…. not yet anyway," chuckled Benedict.

Charlotte's heart raced. She wanted to storm in and see what they were talking about. But she took a calming breath and decided not to jump to conclusions. Instead, she continued to listen before losing her cool.

"Siobhan, this is wrong. It's completely inappropriate," Benedict said. He sounded perplexed, which gave Charlotte a little reassurance.

"I know you are with Charlotte. We shouldn't be doing this. But, come on, just a little more. Please?"

Benedict made an audible sigh before he continued. "You are a truly beautiful woman. I would be lying if I said I wasn't tempted.... if I hadn't.....no, I can't, Siobhan. This is too much. I don't think you should...."

Benedict's words cut off, and no one spoke for a minute. Finally, curiosity got the better of Charlotte, and she peeked around the door. Siobhan clutched Benedict's shirt, and her lips were locked on his. He did not try to pull away.

It was too much for Charlotte. Her world crumbled. She had been betrayed by the man she loved. And with a colleague no less. If word got out—something she was certain Siobhan would tell everyone—she couldn't show her face in the school again. She had been so happy here, and now it was a place tarnished. Her chest felt heavy and sharp with a pain she had never felt before, a pain she never wanted to feel again. Heartbreak. A true love heartbreak. She couldn't hold her emotions back and burst out crying as she raced down the halls.

As she drew closer to the door leading to the car park, she heard Benedict yelling after her. She didn't want to hear anything he had to say. As she closed the door behind her, the last thing she saw was Benedict, his tie askew with Siobhan's lipstick still on his lips.

"DARLING? WHAT'S WRONG?" Ava cried as Charlotte hammered on her mother's door. She pushed past Ava to get inside the moment the door was opened.

Mascara ran tracks down her face, and her hair was unkempt from all the times she had run her fingers through it. Tears had fallen onto her silk blouse, leaving little black mascara stains. "Everything you said is true. He doesn't love me at all. It was all a lie," Charlotte cried.

She flung herself on the plush velvet sofa and hid her face in her hands.

"I'm sure that's not true, darling. What happened?" Ava asked sweetly.

"I don't want to talk about it. But, mum, this pain it's the worst thing I have ever felt. I just want it to go away. I can't go back to that place. Never!" Charlotte howled.

Ava ran over and pulled her daughter into her arms. She said nothing as she held her tight, allowing her to let it all out.

"What happened?" Ava kept asking. She wanted Charlotte to speak it out loud. To make it real.

"I found him in his office with Siobhan. He was kissing her. You should have heard the conversation. It was disgusting!" Charlotte cried.

Ava and Charlotte talked all evening until the early hours of the following day. Charlotte decided. She couldn't go back to school. She couldn't face the humiliation. She typed up her resignation and emailed it immediately to Mrs. Brown. Ava agreed she needed distance from Fernbrook and booked them a train ticket to London for the following evening. Charlotte lined up several gigs for the rest of the month. *If I'm too busy doing modelling gigs, I'm too busy to think. If I'm too busy to think, I will be too busy to feel this pain,* or so she tried to convince herself.

Chapter Twenty-Seven

BENEDICT WANTED to chase after Charlotte, but the look she gave him as she left had him feeling broken. How could he explain what happened? He had to try. He was distracted for the rest of the day, sending her message after message that remained unread. She wasn't picking up her phone. He needed to talk to her, to explain, even if the truth sounded far-fetched. He raced to her house when school ended, but her car wasn't there. She wasn't home. He called and called but got no answer. The next day when he saw her car wasn't in her parking space at school, he knew something was wrong.

"Do you know anything about this?" asked Mrs. Brown, storming into Benedict's office and waving a piece of paper.

Benedict took the paper from her hand and inspected it. It was a printout of the last email Charlotte had sent to her. It was her resignation, effective immediately. Benedict didn't stick around to answer questions. Instead, he jumped to his feet and raced to his car. He drove round to Charlotte's and was immediately thankful her car was still there. He pounded his fist against the door, making as much noise as possible. He knew Charlotte would invite him in if it looked like the neighbours would bear witness to a scene.

"What?" she snapped as she flung open the door.

Benedict froze. Her face was full of fury, and her eyes were cold. She looked like a different person. It pained him to see it.

"What's this? You're resigning?"

"You and Siobhan didn't leave me much choice," she replied, folding her arms and blocking the door.

That she no longer cared if the neighbours saw made him panic. This was not the Charlotte he knew. "Can I come in?"

"No."

"Charlotte, please!"

"I have nothing to say to you." She stepped back and attempted to close the door, but Benedict was fast enough to reach out and stop her.

"Charlotte, nothing happened with Siobhan and me...."

She didn't give him a chance to finish. Either she no longer cared, or she didn't wish to believe him. "I saw you. You still wore her lipstick as you chased me down the halls."

"It's not what it looks like. I promise....and I can prove it," Benedict insisted.

"I'm not interested. Leave me alone," she snapped, pushing as hard as she could to shut the door, but it was useless. Benedict was stronger than her.

"At least let me explain. Then if you don't want to hear from me again, I will leave you alone. I promise."

She stood silently. Waiting.

"Siobhan came to my office. She asked if I would look over a script for the school's next drama performance. She said Mrs. Brown wouldn't approve it without me. I was running lines with her. The script was not appropriate for the school. Its content was too mature. I tried to tell her, and she launched at me," he explained.

Hearing it out loud, even he couldn't believe it. Who would? It sounded like the worst excuse on the planet.

"Even if that were true, you didn't stop her. I stood watching. You never attempted to push her away."

"I don't have an explanation for that. I should have pushed her away faster, but I was in shock."

"This isn't the first time I have found you with her. I can't trust you. Goodbye, *Benedict*," she said, hate dripping from his name.

"This can't be over," he could barely croak the words out.

She said nothing. She waited for him to drop his arm. She stared back, eyes cold as ice. When he no longer held the door, she slammed it in his face.

"I still have the script. It's back in my office. I can prove it. Charlotte, please," he begged, pounding on the door again, but she didn't answer.

He sat in his car for hours. He waited for her to open the door to anyone just so he could talk to her again. Finally, he left only when she messaged, threatening to call the police and have him charged with stalking or harassment.

He wasn't ashamed to admit that he cried on the drive home or that he cried himself to sleep that night. He tossed and turned, trying to make sense of the day's events. How had everything become such a mess? How had he allowed Siobhan to get him in such a position? Could he even blame her? Why hadn't he pushed her away sooner? But the question that caused him the most pain was, what could he do to make Charlotte forgive him?

Chapter Twenty-Eight

BENEDICT prepared to go to work the following morning but felt lost. His body was on autopilot, but his head and heart had switched off. He had dated little over the years and told no one he loved them before. He never imagined what loving someone could feel like until he'd met Charlotte. He had gone from the happiest he had ever been to completely broken in less than twenty-four hours. Food was tasteless, and even when he slammed his thumb in his car door, the pain was nothing compared to the emotional abyss he found himself in. He sat in his office mindlessly staring into his coffee cup, twirling his spoon with no motivation to drink or carry out his day. He just wanted to go back home and curl up in bed. He wanted to call her, go around and break down her door, and beg for her forgiveness.

"Morning," sang a voice outside his door.

It was Siobhan greeting her students. She was practically singing. That she was so happy made Benedict physically sick. How could she be so ecstatic when she had destroyed his life only hours before? Did she know what she was doing? Had she planned it? He had no doubt in his mind that she had. Siobhan was a childish, manipulative gossip of a woman. Drama and pain were like oxygen to her.

He made a note to avoid her all day because he knew if he saw her, he wouldn't be able to control his temper, and the words he wanted to say would surely get him kicked out of the school permanently.

"Benedict, can you cover the English class today? Laura is off sick with flu. I've got a substitute coming but not until eleven. I just need cover for the first period," Mrs. Brown asked.

Benedict never used to mind when Mrs. Brown would walk in without knocking, but today he found it particularly irritating.

"Sure, no problem," he replied.

"Everything OK? "

"No, but I will deal," he mumbled, keeping his eyes fixated on his swirling cup of coffee.

He didn't even hear Mrs. Brown leave.

He checked his phone every chance he got, praying Charlotte would have messaged, but there was nothing. He forced himself not to call her, to respect her wishes to be left alone. But his insides twisted, urging him to fight for her.

He didn't know what to do.

Summer made way to fall, and he hadn't seen or spoken to Charlotte. But she had not left his thoughts for a second. The students had complained to Mrs. Brown that Benedict seemed distant or snapped when they got simple questions wrong. He no longer cared. Not just for teaching, but for anything. He couldn't concentrate but also found he had so much energy that he didn't know what to do with it. He began running at night to try to clear his mind but always found he would run past her house, and his heart would sink when her car wasn't there.

Where was she? Has she moved? The thoughts drove him mad.

"Yo! Can you do me a favour? I need to leave early Thursday. Can you cover my science class? It's for first year so the class should be easy," Simon asked one morning.

"Which science?"

"Chemistry," Simon answered.

Benedict nodded and carried on with his day.

"Is he OK? He hasn't been himself in a while," Benedict heard the teachers gossip.

"I heard the students have complained about him. If he isn't careful, he will lose his job."

He didn't care. As long as they were not gossiping about him and Charlotte, they could say what they wanted.

Thursday arrived in the blink of an eye. Benedict prepared Simon's science lab for the day's last class. He pulled chemicals from the locked cabinet, set up jars of safety glass and placed safety goggles on each table. The students rolled in, and he overheard a group of girls laughing and gossiping. Their words stabbed at him.

"That's why she's not here. She's modelling again. Look, she's due to open Central Faces' *New Faces* runway show at the end of the month. It's all over Facebook."

At least now he knew where she was. Benedict pulled out his phone and searched for the Facebook post. He became so lost in staring at pictures of her, that he wasn't paying attention to the class. In each photo, she smiled back at him, but he could still see the pain in her eyes. He wondered if she still felt the same way if she had any feelings of love left for him at all.

"Sir? When is the class going to start?"

"Oh, yeah, sorry...." Benedict shoved his phone in his pocket and began the lesson.

He had allowed his mind to wander so much he wasn't paying attention when he explained the chemical reactions of certain chemicals. He didn't even know which chemicals he mixed. The last thing he remembered was the liquid turned bright fiery orange and a gas engulfing the room, burning his eyes, and making him and the students struggle to breathe.

"Quick, everyone out!" Benedict yelled.

As the kids ran into the hall, coughing and crying out in distress, he yanked the fire alarm to evacuate the building. As students and teachers gathered on the football field, teachers read off the names of the registers to make sure everyone was present and accounted for. Mrs. Brown called the fire brigade and an ambulance to check over the students. When everything was given the all-clear, she sent the students home.

"What the heck happened?" Mrs. Brown demanded when they were alone together back in her office.

"I don't know, I'm sorry. I mixed up the vials. I don't even know what I mixed," he said apologetically. He felt guilty and worried desperately for the health of the kids.

Mrs. Brown was furious. "That's the problem. You have been absent for weeks now and look what happened. You could have seriously injured these kids. I should fire you on the spot!"

Benedict couldn't blame her. If he was head, he would fire him too. He had become reckless and stupid, and it was no longer just affecting him. He needed to get his head in the game. He needed to think straight, and the only way to do that was to talk to Charlotte.

"Please don't. I know I messed up, and I will personally go to those students' homes and explain what happened to their parents. I will take full responsibility," Benedict pleaded.

"No need to go that far. The kids have all been checked over. They are fine. But you will take responsibility for this. I don't know what has gotten into lately, Benedict, but I've reached my limit. This is your last warning. One more screw-up, and you are out. Do you hear me?" Mrs. Brown yelled.

"I understand. Can I take a few days to get my head straight?"

"I wish you would," Mrs. Brown snapped back, giving Benedict a dismissive wave letting him know she was done with him. For now.

Chapter Twenty-Nine

BENEDICT COULDN'T DENY it any longer. Charlotte's absence from his life was affecting him more than he realised. She had become so ingrained in his every day that the thought of her moving on without him was crushing him. He couldn't think straight. He needed to see her and try one last time to make her see how much he cared for her. She was the best thing to ever happen to him, and he needed to fight for her.

He stalked her social media to try to track down exactly where she was. She had posted only hours before stating the show was being hosted in the 02 Arena in central London, but that wasn't the only news. She had been offered a permanent job in Italy. He felt his stomach drop at the thought. While he was happy that she had been provided such a fantastic opportunity, he felt selfish for not wanting her to leave. He didn't bother telling Mrs. Brown he would not be in before he booked his train ticket and left without a second thought.

On the journey, he thought over what he was going to say. He didn't want to stop her from going if it was what she wanted and if it would make her happy, but he needed her to know how he felt. He also needed to think about getting past Ava. He knew she wouldn't give up her hold over Charlotte without a fight. He also had no idea how he would get past security. But that was an issue for when he arrived.

It was easier than he expected getting past security. He picked the most inexperienced-looking guard—a kid barely out of school. He made up a story about Prada and Gucci getting into an argument about fabric and models. He played his role so well the guard was too flustered to pick apart his story and let him right through.

He searched dressing room after dressing room before he came across Ava. Charlotte was nowhere in sight.

"What are you doing here?" Ava snarled; she sat in Charlotte's makeup chair like she owned the place.

"I'm here to speak to Charlotte. Where is she?" he asked, purposefully not making eye contact.

"She's not here. You are too late," she replied, checking her nails with a smug, self-satisfied look. "I suggest you leave before I call security."

"I got past them once, I can do it again. I'm not leaving without talking to her," he insisted, taking a seat on the sofa behind the door.

"She told me about what happened and the story you told, trying to explain it all away. I held her while she cried," Ava began standing and slowly pacing the room to irritate and intimidate him.

He tried to keep his face expressionless, but he knew she saw the heartache in his eyes. The thought of Charlotte crying because of him cut deep. Like a paper cut to the heart, it stung.

"She almost believed you too. I convinced her otherwise, of course. Getting Siobhan to dispose of the scripts certainly took care of that," she said, leaning down to fix her makeup in the mirror.

Benedict sat up at attention. He should have known Ava had something to do with it. He knew she was a manipulator and had her own agenda. Still, he never imagined she could be so evil, or so cold and heartless. To cause her daughter such pain and clearly have no ounce of remorse. It was sickening.

"Come again?" he said in disbelief. Of course he'd heard her just fine. But he also knew what an egotist Ava was, and if he gave her enough room, she would brag about her victory.

"Did you think Siobhan was smart enough to come up with that little charade all on her own? She thinks she's something else, but let's face it, the girl is dense. No, it had to be convincing. A story so ludicrous no one would believe such an unreasonable explanation," Ava bragged.

"Why would you do that?" Benedict asked in shock, not believing a mother would do that to her child.

"You. As long as you were in the picture, Charlotte fought against me. But the doors that girl can open with her modelling are phenomenal. Because of her, my pageant girls are flourishing, and I've been able to double my prices. I was struggling for a long time. I was worried I would go broke, but that's all changed. And now, with this Italy job, I too can expand," Ava said, smiling like she had won the lottery.

"How can you use her like that? She's your own daughter!" Benedict felt sick just listening to her. "You don't deserve her. She's worth ten of you. I just wish she could see what a monster you are. All she ever wanted was a normal mother-daughter relationship with you!" Benedict yelled, his anger growing with every word that left Ava's lips.

"Oh, please. Do you know what I gave up for that girl? What I lost? She owes me," Ava spat.

Just then, Charlotte walked in, tear stains down her face, anger and pain in her eyes.

"I owe you nothing! I should have known you would never change. You vile, self-centred witch!" Charlotte said, her tone simple yet filled with bile and disgust.

"Charlotte.... I...." Ava stuttered, unable to think of a response to finally being caught in the act.

"Don't! I'm done listening to your lies. I'm done being your excuse for being a vile human being. Get out. Out of my dressing room and out of my life." Charlotte said calmly, moving closer to Ava so she could see the sincerity in her daughter's expression.

"Darling..."

"Get out!" Charlotte finally yelled, causing Ava's mouth to fall open in shock.

She didn't move, still expecting Charlotte to change her mind. But when Charlotte didn't so much as flinch, Ava packed her things and slowly left. Finally, Ava walked out of Charlotte's life for good.

Charlotte let her shoulders sag, breathing out a long breath before crumbling against the table in front of the mirror. Benedict was right there for her. He wrapped his arms around her and let her cry out the heartbreak of her mother's betrayal.

"I'm so sorry I didn't believe you," Charlotte whispered, almost as if she feared how Benedict would react.

"You don't need to apologise," he replied, squeezing her tighter, not wanting to ever let her go again.

"Wait, why are you here?"

"Yes, I saw on social media about Italy. I didn't want you to leave without me telling you how I really feel." He smiled.

Absence makes the heart grow fonder. The distance between Benedict and Charlotte, because of Ava, was precisely what they needed to see how much they were meant to be. Charlotte was never one to let anyone down and carried on with the show that fateful night, but respectfully turned down the job in Italy. Ava tried several times to get back in touch. Still, when Charlotte put out a video to her fans about why she was leaving modelling for good – and talked openly about just how toxic her relationship was with Ava – the attempts for contact stopped. Ava finally left her daughter alone.

Mrs. Brown quickly ripped up Charlotte's resignation and accepted her back with open arms, as did the students. Everyone was glad to see her back in The Northern Swan doing what she meant to do: help people.

Siobhan left not long after Charlotte's return. Charlotte was a good person and didn't name Siobhan in her social media post, but guilt has a way of eating away at you. The guilt and shame were too much for Siobhan. The last thing Charlotte heard was she had taken a job in Manchester as a drama instructor.

Epilogue

TWO YEARS LATER

BENEDICT AND CHARLOTTE'S relationship went from good to better, and within a year, Charlotte moved in with Benedict. They made each other into better versions of themselves. When Mrs. Brown accepted a job at another school, Benedict happily accepted the promotion as head teacher. By popular demand from both students and the other teachers, Charlotte was voted the best choice for the following role of deputy headteacher.

The Northern Swan won at the science fair for the next two years, and Benedict and Charlotte's love affair was featured in an article in the local news. The world fell in love with the story of childhood enemies turned lovers who helped the school that brought them together. The Northern Swan was inundated with investors and applications from new students, and Benedict and Charlotte had received awards for head teacher team of the year two years running.

"Hey Charlotte, how are you?" asked Simon when he joined her in the staff room.

"I'm wonderful, absolutely wonderful!" She beamed.

Charlotte was busting at the seams. She carried around a secret with her for days. News that would change everything in the best possible way. She wanted to scream it from the rooftops, but she had a plan first.

"Date night tonight?" Simon asked.

"Yep, second anniversary." She couldn't stop smiling.

VIVA LA MEXICO had been their go-to place for celebrations after their first date; it held so many memories that Benedict and Charlotte just wanted to keep adding more. Their second anniversary was no exception. Charlotte dressed in a black pencil skirt and white silk blouse with a gold belt, reminiscent of her first day at the school and the first time in fifteen years that they had seen each other. The metaphor was not lost on him.

Benedict looked a picture of handsomeness and the image of a man madly in love with his girlfriend. Arm in arm, they strode inside and sat at their regular table by the window, enjoying a beautiful three-course meal, reminiscing over their time together. While most people would say the honeymoon period fades, with Benedict and Charlotte, the spark was just as bright, if not stronger, than it had been on day one.

"I have something I want to ask you." Charlotte grinned, her hands shaking slightly under the table as she fidgeted with her napkin. Not out of nerves, but excitement.

"What a coincidence, I have a question for you too." Benedict winked. "Ladies first."

"No, mine can wait, you first!" She blushed.

"OK," Benedict said, tugging at his neckline nervously. "I had this big speech prepared. I pictured this big moment that had to be some-thing spectacular. Something to remember. But as always, with you, I have so much I could say I get lost for words." Watching her, he noticed how a knowing grin slowly spread across her face.

"Then I thought, it doesn't matter what I say because you already know. You can read my mind and know me better than I know myself. So, I thought there is nothing I could do to make this moment better than to just ask you." He stopped and reached into his jacket pocket and dropped to one knee.

"Char, will you do me the honour of making me even happier than I am right now....and be my wife?"

The tables nearby watched in awe, clinking spoons against glasses and waiting silently for her response. Then, finally, the room was so silent you could hear a pin drop.

"Yes," she chuckled, wrapping herself around him and kissing him with a kiss steeped in love, happiness, and the promise of the best life together.

The room erupted in applause while the waiters rushed over with a gigantic bouquet of roses, the perfect mix of red, white, and yellow, and a bottle of champagne. Benedict had guessed her ring size, but luckily the marquise cut halo white gold ring with ruby shoulders fit perfectly.

"I love you," she breathed as they sat back down.

"I love you more," he replied, holding her hand across the table.

"You said you had a question for me?" Benedict said, picking up his champagne and taking a sip after toasting her. Charlotte smiled, taking a sip of her water.

"I do.... what do you think of the name Charlie.... for a boy or girl?" she asked with a grin.

It took Benedict a few seconds before the light bulb went off in his head. Gently he placed his glass back down. His lips broke out in a smile that touched his eyes. "Are you? Are we?" he stuttered.

She chuckled. "I'm pregnant!"

"I'm going to be a father?"

"The best," she replied smiling.

Benedict jumped out of his chair and ran around, scooping her up in his arms and twirling her around. The nearby patrons laughed, admiring the love the pair shared.

"This is the best night of my life. She said yes, and I'm going to be a dad," Benedict announced his happiness to the entire restaurant, then kissed her to the cheers and applause of those around them.

The End
Did you enjoy *Extra Credit*?
Please consider rating it on Goodreads, or Bookbub, or your favorite retailer. Reviews help me reach new readers.

Join my Newsletter at www.daisylandishromance.com for new releases, sales and giveaways!

About the Author

Daisy Landish is a clean romance and cozy mystery author whose clean and sweet novellas have tugged at readers' heartstrings around the world. When she's not writing love stories, Daisy spends her time reading, hiking at dawn, and riding into the sunset on her horse, Rosebud.

www.daisylandishromance.com

facebook.com/daisylandishromance

x.com/daisy_landish

instagram.com/daisylandishbooks

amazon.com/author/daisylandish

bookbub.com/authors/daisy-landish

goodreads.com/Daisy_Landish

Also by Daisy Landish

Clean Regency Romance

Christmas with the Earl

The Lady Series - The Allington Collection

The Lady Series - The Gillingham Collection

The Lady Series - The Blackmore Collection

The Lady Series - The Norrington Collection

Clean Contemporary Romance

Timeline Retreats

Maplewood Grove Series

Love on Spruce Island

Second Chance

Cherry Tree Island

The Wedding Trio

Extra Credit

Counting on the Cowboy

Focusing on the Cowboy

Mistletoe Magic

Grounded at Christmas

Cozy Mysteries

Sophie Brooks Mysteries

Jane and Kennedy Daniels Mysteries

Pine Grove Mysteries

Annie Archer Paranormal Mysteries

Wilma Wade Holiday Mysteries

Mike and Maddie Mysteries